"Unfortunately, the [gift comes] with a condition—which is that I must be married in order to inherit. And although the very idea is abhorrent to me, I want that piece of land for my people," Zayed said, his voice growing deep with fervor. "So much so, that I'm prepared to marry in order to get it."

"Then why not ask one of your many girlfriends?" Jane questioned archly.

"Because I don't want love and I don't wish to be tied to one woman—at least not until it is time for me to produce an heir. The union I propose with you will be nothing other than a means to an end. A brief union, which I intend to dissolve after six months."

She looked at him curiously. "On what grounds?"

"Non-consummation, of course." He shrugged his powerful shoulders.

Jane nodded, her heart pounding painfully against her rib cage, her mind working over the facts as she pieced together the intention behind his bizarre request. "So you decided to pick a woman to whom you were not in the least bit attracted?"

"Exactly." He sat back in his chair, his black eyes lasering into her.

"And I am that woman."

"You most certainly are. I cannot think of a more ideal candidate."

Wedlocked!

Conveniently wedded, passionately bedded!

Whether there's a debt to be paid, a will
to be obeyed or a business to be saved...
she's got no choice but to say "I do!"

But these billionaire bridegrooms have got
another think coming if they imagine marriage
will be that easy...

Soon their convenient brides become
the objects of an *inconvenient* desire!

Find out what happens after the vows in

The Billionaire's Defiant Acquisition by Sharon Kendrick

One Night to Wedding Vows by Kim Lawrence

Wedded, Bedded, Betrayed by Michelle Smart

Expecting a Royal Scandal by Caitlin Crews

Trapped by Vialli's Vows by Chantelle Shaw

Baby of His Revenge by Jennie Lucas

A Diamond for Del Rio's Housekeeper by Susan Stephens

Bound by His Desert Diamond by Andie Brock

Bride by Royal Decree by Caitlin Crews

Claimed for the De Carrillo Twins by Abby Green

The Desert King's Captive Bride by Annie West

Look out for more **Wedlocked!** stories
coming soon!

Sharon Kendrick

THE SHEIKH'S BOUGHT WIFE

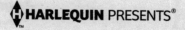

HARLEQUIN PRESENTS®

Recycling programs
for this product may
not exist in your area.

ISBN-13: 978-0-373-06061-0

The Sheikh's Bought Wife

First North American Publication 2017

Copyright © 2017 by Sharon Kendrick

www.Harlequin.com

Printed in U.S.A.

Sharon Kendrick once won a national writing competition by describing her ideal date: being flown to an exotic island by a gorgeous and powerful man. Little did she realize that she'd just wandered into her dream job! Today she writes for Harlequin, featuring often stubborn but always to-die-for heroes and the women who bring them to their knees. She believes that the best books are those you never want to end. Just like life...

Books by Sharon Kendrick

Harlequin Presents

A Royal Vow of Convenience
The Ruthless Greek's Return
Christmas in Da Conti's Bed
The Sheikh's Undoing

One Night With Consequences

Secrets of a Billionaire's Mistress
Crowned for the Prince's Heir
Carrying the Greek's Heir

The Billionaire's Legacy

Di Sione's Virgin Mistress

Wedlocked!

The Billionaire's Defiant Acquisition

The Bond of Billionaires

Claimed for Makarov's Baby
The Sheikh's Christmas Conquest

At His Service

The Housekeeper's Awakening

Desert Men of Qurhah

Defiant in the Desert
Shamed in the Sands
Seduced by the Sultan

Visit the Author Profile page at Harlequin.com for more titles.

To the fabulous Janie Heard—supersharp judge, sublime interpreter of Ottolenghi recipes, musician, most prolific reader in the book club and possessor of an earthy sense of humor.

Thanks for all your advice on the legal aspects of marital consummation—which provided an interesting and hilarious correspondence.

PROLOGUE

'So what's the catch?'

Zayed detected the faint ripple of unease which ran through his advisors as he shot out his silky question. They were nervous, he could tell. More nervous than was usual in the presence of a sheikh of his power and influence. Not that he cared about their nerves. On the contrary, he found them useful. Deference and fear kept people at a distance and that was exactly where he liked them.

Turning away from the window which overlooked his magnificent palace gardens, he studied the men who stood in front of him—the guileless expression on the face of his closest aide, Hassan, not fooling him for a moment.

'*Catch*, Your Most Supreme Highness?' questioned Hassan.

'Yes, catch,' Zayed echoed, his voice growing impatient now. 'My maternal grandfather has died and I discover he has gifted me one of the most valuable pieces of land in the entire desert region. Inheriting Dahabi Makaan was something which never even entered my mind.' He frowned. 'Which leaves me wondering what has prompted this gesture of unexpected generosity.'

Hassan gave a slight bow. 'Because you are one of his few remaining blood relatives, sire, and thus surely such a bequest is perfectly natural.'

'That much may be true,' Zayed conceded. 'But until recently he had not spoken to me since I was a boy of seven summers.'

'Your grandfather was undoubtedly touched by your visit as he lay on his deathbed—a visit he must surely not have been anticipating,' said Hassan diplomatically. 'Perhaps that is the reason.'

Zayed's jaw tightened. Perhaps it was. But the visit had not been inspired by love, since love had long departed from his heart. He had gone because duty had demanded it and Zayed never shirked from duty. He had gone despite the fierce pain it had caused him to do so. And yes, it had been a strange sensation to look upon the ravaged face of the old king, who had cut off his only daughter after her marriage to Zayed's father. But death was the great equaliser, he remembered thinking bitterly as the gnarled old fingers had clutched at his. The stealthy foe from which no man or woman could ever escape. He had made his peace with his dying grandfather because he suspected it would have pleased his mother for him to do so, not because he'd been seeking some kind of financial reward.

'Nobody gives something for nothing in this world, but perhaps this is an exception.' Zayed's eyes bored questioningly into those of his aide. 'Are you telling me that the land is to be mine, without condition?'

Hassan hesitated and the pause which followed sounded heavy. Ominous. 'Not quite.'

Zayed nodded. So his unerring instinct had not failed him after all! 'You mean there *is* a catch,' he said triumphantly.

Hassan nodded. 'I suspect that you will see it as one, sire—for in order to inherit Dahabi Makaan, you need to be...' nervously, he licked his lips '...married.'

'Married?' echoed Zayed, his voice deepening with a dangerous note, which made the aides shoot glances of increasing anxiety at each other.

'Yes, sire.'

'You know my feelings about marriage.'

'Indeed, sire.'

'But just so there can be no misunderstanding, I will reiterate them for you. I have no desire to marry—at least, not for many years. Why tie yourself to one woman when you can enjoy twenty?' Zayed gave a fleeting smile as he remembered visit-

ing his mistress in New York last week and the sight
of her lying on rumpled satin sheets clad in nothing but a tight black basque, her milky thighs open
and welcoming. He cleared his throat and willed the
hardening in his groin to subside. 'I accept that one
day I will need to provide my kingdom with an heir
and that is the moment when I shall take a bride—
a pure young virgin from my own kingdom. A moment which will not come for many decades, for a
man can procreate until he is sixty, seventy—in some
cases, even eighty. And since I believe it is the modern way for young women to enjoy all the expertise
of an older lover, it will be a highly satisfactory arrangement for both participants.'

Hassan nodded. 'I understand your reasoning en-
tirely, sire, and usually I would completely concur
with your judgment. But this land is priceless. It is
oil rich and of huge strategic significance. Think
how much it could benefit your people if it were to
be yours.'

Zayed felt indignation heat his blood. Didn't he
spend almost all his waking hours thinking about
his people and how to do his best by them? Was he
not the most successful of all the desert Sheikhs because of his dedication to his land and his determination to be a peacekeeper? And yet Hassan's words
were true. Dahabi Makaan would undoubtedly be a
glittering jewel in the crown of his kingdom. Could

he really turn his back on such a proposition? His mouth flattened. He remembered his dying grandfather croaking out a plea for him not to leave it too long to produce an heir, so that their bloodline could continue. And when Zayed had coolly remarked that he had no intention of marrying for many years, the old man's face had crumpled. Had the wily old king decided that the only way to achieve his heart's desire was to force the issue, by making marriage a condition of the inheritance?

Yet the thought of marriage made Zayed want to recoil. To turn away from its insidious tentacles, which could bind a man in so many ways. He loathed marriage for more reasons than a high libido which demanded variety. He loathed the institution of marriage with all its flaws and baseless promises and the very idea of finding a bride in order to inherit was something which repulsed every fibre of his being.

Unless…

His mind began to pick over the possibilities— because wouldn't only a fool turn down the chance to be master of a region renowned for the black gold known as oil, as well as its prized position straddling four desert countries?

'Perhaps there is a way in which the conditions of the will could be met,' he said slowly, 'and yet not tie me into all the tedium and inconvenience of a long-term marriage.'

'You know of such a way, sire?' questioned Hassan. 'Pray, enlighten us, oh, knowledgeable one.'

'If the marriage were not to be *consummated*,' Zayed continued thoughtfully, 'then it would not be legal and, as such, could quickly be dissolved. Is that not so?'

'But, sire—'

'No buts,' said Zayed impatiently. 'For the idea grows on me with every second which passes.' Yet he could see the look of doubt on his aide's face and knew very well what had caused it. Because Zayed was a man known for his virility. A man who needed the regular release of sex in order to sustain him—in the same way that a horse needed oats and exercise in order to live. He doubted there was a woman alive who could resist him in her bed and the idea that he could tolerate a sexless marriage was almost laughable. Yes, there were undeniably obstacles to such a chaste union but Zayed was a man who thrived on overcoming obstacles, and as he stared into Hassan's perplexed face a brilliant idea began to form in his mind.

'What if I were to choose a woman who does not tempt me in any way?' he said slowly. 'A drab woman who makes a mockery of all that is feminine. A woman who would turn a blind eye if I happened to stray. Surely that would provide the perfect solution?'

'You know of such a woman, sire?'

Zayed's mouth flattened into a hard line. Oh, yes. He knew of such a woman. An image swam into his mind as he thought about Jane Smith who, with her mousy hair and the colourless clothes which swamped her figure, fitted the bill perfectly. What was it that the English said about a woman on whom the gods had not gifted much in the way of looks? *Plain Jane.* Yes, indeed. Never had such a description been truer than of the uptight academic who was in charge of the archives of his embassy in London. For not only was she plain, she was also immune to his charms, some might even say *disapproving*—a fact he had registered a while back with something approaching incredulity. At first he'd thought she must be playing games with him. That she was using that well-known feminine ploy of affecting indifference towards a powerful man, in the hope that it would stir some interest in his groin and in his heart. As if any part of him could ever be stirred by Jane Smith! He had discovered her attitude to be real and not feigned when he'd overheard someone mentioning his name and, as he had silently rounded the corner of his London embassy, had seen her rolling her eyes. Insolent, foolish woman!

Yet Jane loved his country with a passion which was rare for a foreigner and she knew it better than many of its natives, which was why he hadn't instantly dismissed her for gross insubordination. She adored every contour of its deserts, its palaces and its rich, sometimes bloody history. Zayed's heart gave a savage wrench of pain. A pain which had never quite healed no matter how hard he had tried to turn his back on it. Might not it help that healing process if he accepted his grandfather's bequest and acquired Dahabi Makaan? To close a door on the past and to look beyond, to the future?

'Prepare my jet, Hassan,' he said harshly. 'And I will fly to England to take the wretched Jane Smith as my bride.'

CHAPTER ONE

THE DAY HAD started out badly for Jane and now it seemed it was going to get a whole lot worse. First there had been the phone call—one of the ominous and highly disturbing phone calls which had started arriving daily, leaving her feeling frustrated and scared. Then her train had broken down on her way into work, where she was greeted by complete panic by the time she arrived at the Kafalah Embassy. And the news which awaited her made her heart sink. Sheikh Zayed Al Zawba had decided to pay an unexpected flying visit—quite literally, since he was currently on board his private jet and expected within the next couple of hours. He was a proud and demanding man and the ambassador had been nervously barking out instructions left, right and centre while every female secretary had been grinning as they eagerly awaited the arrival of the desert king, because Zayed was also known for an arrogant charm and sex appeal which made women flock to him like moths to the light bulb. But Jane grimaced when she heard of his impending arrival. She banged her office door shut more loudly than was necessary because she didn't think he was charming or sexy. She didn't care that he was a wizard when it came to negotiating trade settlements, or building schools and hospitals in his homeland.

She hated him.

She hated the way his black eyes glittered whenever he talked to you as if he were in possession of some secret he wasn't going to let you in on. She hated the way women reacted whenever he was around—fawning all over him as if he were some kind of god. A sex god, she'd once overheard someone whisper. She swallowed. Because wasn't that what she hated most of all—the fact that she wasn't immune to the undeniable allure of the desert Sheikh, even though he represented everything she most despised—with his legions of lovers and his callous disregard for the feelings of the opposite sex? And yes, she knew he'd had a pretty awful upbringing—but did that give him *carte blanche* to behave exactly as he liked? How long were you supposed to make allowances for the past?

Hanging up her jacket, she tucked the back of her blouse into her skirt and sat down at her desk. At least her office was hidden away in the shadowed basement of the Central London embassy, far away from the excitement of the gilded upstairs and all the preparations which were being made for Zayed's arrival. With a bit of luck she could hide herself away down here and not even *see* him.

Automatically she switched on her computer and the screen immediately lit up with a beautiful screen-saver of the famous palace of Kafalah but unusually, Jane saw nothing. For once the blue dome and gilded arches failed to register because all she could think about was the phone call she'd received first thing this morning and the now-familiar voice of the man making it. The message he gave was simple and didn't vary but the tone of his voice was becoming increasingly hostile. She didn't know how he'd got hold of her number—all she could think about was the growing note of threat each time she spoke to him. This morning he had got straight to the point.

'Your sister owes a lot of money and somebody needs to pay. Is that somebody going to be you, sweetheart—because I'm getting kind of impatient?'

The line went dead and Jane could have bent her head down over her keyboard and wept—except she wasn't the kind of person who ever allowed herself the luxury of tears. Crying was a waste of time and she wasn't about to start now, because she was Jane the coper. Jane who everyone else turned to when they were in trouble. Jane who could always be relied upon when the chips were down and the world around was dissolving into chaos. Because years ago she'd stumbled upon a certain truth – that if there was a problem then it could be sorted, if only you looked hard enough to find a solution.

Pulling her mobile phone from her handbag, she clicked onto Cleo's number but it went straight through to the answering service and she got the drawled message which was supposed to be funny—only right now it didn't sound remotely funny.

'Hi, this is Cleo. Leave a message and I might call you back. But then again, I might not.'

Jane took a deep breath and tried to keep calm even though her heart was crashing against her rib-cage in a way which was making breathing difficult. 'Cleo, this is Jane and I need to speak to you. Like now. Could you either pick up if you're listening, or call me back as soon as you get this?'

But Cleo didn't pick up and, as she cut the con-nection, Jane didn't hold out much hope that her sis-ter would call back. Cleo was a law unto herself and lately that law seemed to have no boundaries. As non-identical twins they shared the same birthday—but that was just about all they shared. Jane loved the safety and stimulation of books while Cleo liked dancing the night away. Jane dressed for comfort—Cleo for show. Cleo was beautiful and Jane was not.

But Cleo's lifestyle couldn't possibly be financed by the money she earned only erratically, though her spending hadn't taken that into account. Why else would some bailiff-type person have got hold of Jane's number and started making all kinds of threats if her twin didn't pay back some of her mounting debts? She decided to phone her after work, maybe even go and see her—and she would stand over her sister until she made an appointment to see her bank manager and sorted out this whole sorry mess.

With an effort, Jane pushed Cleo's troubles out of her mind as she began to focus on what needed to be done and soon her mind was clear of debt and menace and a world she didn't want to be part of. That was one of the many things she loved about her work as an academic, specialising in the desert kingdom of Kafalah. You could spirit yourself away into a land rich with culture and history. You could lose yourself in the past. What better way to spend your days than by cataloguing books, or overseeing exhibitions of the fabulous artwork which had emerged from that beautiful country? How much more satisfying than a modern world with which she seemed to have no real connection.

She was completely lost in the translation of an ancient Kafalahian love poem and struggling to find an appropriate word for a decidedly erotic act, when she heard the door open. Making a minor click of irritation beneath her breath, she didn't even bother lifting her head.

'Not now,' she said. 'Come back later.'

There was a moment of complete silence before a silky male voice spoke.

'In my country I would not tolerate such a response to the arrival of the Sheikh,' he said. 'Do you consider yourself so special and different that you should ignore him, Jane Smith?'

The realisation of just who was speaking broke into her deliberations like ice water being tipped over her head and Jane looked up in horror to see that Zayed Al Zawba had entered her office and was shutting the door behind him, enclosing the two of them together in a too-small space. She knew she ought to rise to her feet and bow her head, because even though she wasn't one of his subjects his royal status demanded she show *some* kind of deference even if secretly she objected to it. But her body was refusing to obey the dictates of her mind—maybe because the sight of him was short-circuiting the common sense which usually came to her as easily as breathing. Her mouth dried as his powerful body dominated every atom of space in the room and she cursed him for the way he looked. For the way he made her feel. As if she were clutching onto the edge of a cliff by her fingertips as the unsteady ground beneath began to slip away from her frantic grip.

He was wearing robes. Of course he was. She knew of some visiting sheikhs who adapted their appearance for their time in England by wearing cosmopolitan suits—usually handmade in Italy. But not Zayed. Zayed didn't try to *blend in* to his environment. He liked to stand out and he managed it effortlessly. Flowing cream silk hinted at the hard and sinewy body beneath and his only compromise was leaving his dark head bare.

Her eyes travelled reluctantly to his face. His cruel and beautiful face. Jane had studied generations of Al Zawba men during her time as an academic. She had seen their distinctive features staring down from ancient paintings and illustrations and their flashing black eyes, burnished copper skin and hawk-like nose were all too familiar to her. But nothing could prepare you for seeing all that proud and haughty lineage in the flesh and every time she had encountered Zayed, his impact on her had never lessened— if anything it had only increased. Maybe that wasn't so surprising given his physical magnificence, which she would have been a fool to deny.

But she didn't like the way he made her feel any more than she liked him. It was highly inconvenient that he had only to look at her and her breasts started aching and all she could do was pray that her cheeks didn't display the heated blood which was suddenly pumping furiously around her system. She just needed to maintain her cool—the way she did with every other person she came in contact with.

To politely enquire why he had arrived in her office so unexpectedly—only not so politely that he might feel he could start making a *habit* of it. And then, hopefully, to get rid of him as quickly as possible.

Awkwardly she rose to her feet, aware of those flashing black eyes whipping over her as briefly she bowed her head.

'Forgive me, Your Serene Highness,' she said. 'I was not expecting you to walk in unannounced.'

Zayed raised his eyebrows. Was that *censure* he heard in her soft English voice? 'Should I perhaps have made an appointment first?' he questioned sarcastically. 'Checked up to see whether or not you had time to fit me into your busy schedule?'

The answering gesture of her hand as it encompassed the book-cluttered room was expansive but he noticed that her smile was thin.

'I would have tidied up first, if I had known that Your Royal Highness was going to grace my office with his presence.'

It was on the tip of his tongue to suggest that she might have tidied up her own person as well as her office, but he recognised that such honesty would do little to further his cause. 'The untidy state of your office is of no consequence to me at the moment,' he said impatiently. 'It is you I have come to see.'

'Oh?'

She was looking at him with question in her eyes—

in a way which somehow managed to be deeply insubordinate, though he couldn't quite work out why. He wasn't used to women staring at him like that—as if they would prefer he was anywhere other than here. He was used to adoration and submission—and from women far more beautiful than the one standing in front of him. He had intended to walk in here and tell her that he needed a wife—and quickly—but Jane Smith's faintly hostile expression was making him reconsider as suddenly the unthinkable occurred to him.

What if she refused?

Zayed's mind raced. Refusal was something he would not countenance but perhaps he might have to employ a little good old-fashioned diplomacy along the way. And yet wasn't it slightly ironic that he should have to go creeping around to ask for a favour from a woman like her?

His lips curved as he noticed she wasn't wearing a scrap of make-up and that her brown hair was scraped tightly back into a bun more befitting a woman of fifty than one in her twenties. An ugly blouse was tucked into an equally ugly skirt which fell in an unflattering length to just below her knees and, as always, it was impossible to see what kind of body lay beneath her drab clothes. She was undoubtedly the most unattractive female he had ever set eyes on and thus the perfect candidate for what he had in mind. Could he ever imagine being sexually attracted to a woman like Jane Smith? Not in a million years.

'I have a proposition to put to you,' he said.

Her eyes became hooded as she looked at him warily. 'What kind of proposition?'

Zayed could barely restrain his click of displeasure. How insolent she was! Did she not realise that his power was all-encompassing? Why wasn't she nodding her head in instant agreement—eager to please him in whatever it was he demanded? The loud clicking of a clock on the wall penetrated his thoughts as he became aware of the street view from the basement window. It suddenly occurred to him that laying out his terms for her brief tenure as his Sheikha might be better done elsewhere—not here in this cluttered office with embassy staff nervously patrolling the corridor outside, waiting for his next command or perhaps listening, with their ears pressed close to the door.

Injecting his tone with a deliberate silkiness, Zayed gave a rare smile, aware of its powerful impact on members of the opposite sex. 'It might be easier to explain over dinner.'

'Dinner?'

'You know?' His patience was wearing thin. 'The meal you eat between lunch and breakfast.'

'You want to have dinner?' She frowned. 'With *me*?'

Now was not the time to tell her that no, he didn't,

not really. That the shared meal would be nothing more than something to be endured while he told her what he had planned for her. But why ruin what was undoubtedly going to be the night of a lifetime for her? Why not dazzle her as women so loved to be dazzled?

'Yes,' he said softly. 'I do.'

She screwed up her face. 'I don't understand.'

'But you will, Jane. You will. All will be explained in due course. So.' Lifting his arm so that the fine material of his robe revealed one hair-roughened wrist, he glanced down at the heavy gold timepiece which his father had once worn. 'You had better leave now.'

She stared at him blankly. 'You mean, leave work?'

'Of course.'

'But I've only just got here. And I'm deep into research about a sixteenth century Kafalahian love poem which has just come to light.' She brightened up at this point. 'It was actually written by one of your ancestors to the most favoured member of his harem.'

He was beginning to get irritated now. Didn't she realise the great honour which was being afforded to her? Did she think he asked out women like her every night of the week—and that he would tolerate being turned down so that she could *read a poem*? 'You are having dinner with the leader of the country for whom you work—not grabbing a sandwich in a nearby café!' he bit out. 'And doubtless you will wish to prepare yourself. For not only is this an honour for a member of my staff, it is also supposed to be a treat.'

'A treat?' she echoed doubtfully.

'Indeed. I don't imagine you frequent the capital's high spots every night of the week.'

'I'm not really a "high spot" sort of person,' she said stubbornly.

'No. I can tell.' Fleetingly, Zayed thought her reaction might be almost amusing if it weren't so insulting. But she would soon learn to be grateful. 'I will send a car for you shortly before eight. Make sure you're ready.'

She opened her mouth as if she was about to say something else but maybe something in his eyes stopped her for she nodded, even though her expression made her look as if she'd been asked to do some sort of penance. In fact, he was almost certain that she'd just stifled a resigned kind of *sigh*.

'Very well, Your Royal Highness,' she said stiffly. 'I will be ready just before eight.'

CHAPTER TWO

HER MOBILE PHONE clamped tightly to her ear, Jane
paced up and down in her small sitting room as she
willed her sister to answer. She had been trying in
vain to get hold of her all day—ever since she'd been
forced to leave work early in order to *prepare* herself
for a dinner date she didn't want with the arrogant
Sheikh. An arrangement which was still puzzling her
as she couldn't work out why he should want to spend
time with *her,* since she was confident that the work
she did for him and his country was of the highest
possible standard. And especially since he made no
attempt to hide the fact that he found her company
about as appealing as she found his.

But an evening with Zayed was far less worry-
ing than the two calls she hadn't dared pick up, from
the same number as the man with the threatening
voice who'd called this morning. Suddenly Jane's
safe and contained world felt as if it were spinning
out of control.

'Hello?' The connection clicked and a cautious female voice came onto the line. 'Is that you, Jane?'

Cleo! At last. 'Who else did you think it would be?' Jane questioned, drawing in a grateful breath as she heard her sister's sexy voice. 'What's going on? Why have I been getting threatening phone calls on your behalf from some man who says you owe money?'

There was a pause. A disturbingly long pause from her normally garrulous sister. For a moment she thought the connection had been lost before a single word split the silence.

'Hell.'

Something in the delivery of that word sent a shiver of apprehension quivering down Jane's spine. 'Cleo? Are you going to start telling me what's going on?'

Cleo began to speak, a little hesitantly at first— and then it all came out in a babble which seemed perilously close to tears. And Jane felt she could have written the script herself, because it was all so predictable. Her dizzy, impractical twin sister, whose big dreams had always been way too big, had decided to start living those dreams. Inspired by too much time spent monitoring the lives of minor celebrities on social media, her out-of-control spending had ended in a pile of debts which looked now like mountains.

'Can't you go and speak to your bank manager?'

said Jane, trying to keep her voice steady. 'And pay the money back in instalments?'

There was a hollow kind of laugh in response. 'It's gone beyond that. If I'd borrowed from the bank in the first place, maybe. But I didn't. I borrowed from a man down the pub. Turned out he's a loan shark.'

'Oh, Cleo? *Why?*'

There was a pause. 'Because he was willing to lend to me—why else? I'm not like you, Jane. I don't think everything through to within an inch of its life. I don't spend my life wading through dusty text-books and wearing thrift shop clothes and letting life pass me by. So I...' Cleo's voice faltered. 'I decided I wanted to see the world. I went on a fancy cruise and bought myself a wardrobe to match and I...'

'You pretended to be someone you weren't,' said Jane slowly, because this was a familiar pattern going right back to their childhood. Gorgeous Cleo who wanted to be a famous model—only she wasn't quite tall enough or thin enough. Cleo who had been the apple of their mother's eye. Who had been so devastated when Mum died that everyone had gone out of their way to cushion her from the tearing pain of her emotions. Maybe they had tried too hard, Jane conceded now. Made too many allowances. Bailed her out one time too many. Accepted with a resigned shrug when Cleo dropped out of yet another course and just gone ahead and enrolled her on another—as if they were all waiting for some magic solution to fix her life for her. It had become even worse after their father had died and Jane had been left feeling like the responsible one, the one who needed to take care of Cleo. But that was the story of her life, wasn't it? Everyone leaned on Jane. Good old reliable Jane.

Closing her eyes, she pressed the phone against her ear. 'How much do you owe, Cleo? And I don't want rough estimates designed to shield me from the truth. How much *exactly*?'

The sum her sister mentioned made Jane feel quite sick and for a minute she actually thought her knees might give way. 'You're kidding?' she questioned hoarsely.

'I wish I was. Oh, Jane, what am I going to *do*?'

It was an all too familiar cry and what could Jane do but respond to it, as she had responded so many times before? Tightly, she gripped her phone. 'You're going to sit tight and wait for me to get back to you.'

'But you haven't got that kind of money.'

'No. I haven't.' Jane swallowed as an image of Zayed's face swam before her eyes—all flashing black eyes and cruel, mocking lips. 'But I know somebody who does.'

Slowly, she put the phone down. Did she dare ask the impossibly wealthy Sheikh for some kind of loan to help tide her sister over? A loan which she could pay back over the next however many years?

She was so lost in thought that she didn't realise the time until she heard the clock chime out seven times and realised that Zayed's car would be here in less than an hour.

Dashing into the shower, she sluiced tepid water over her fleshy body realising that she'd been so worried about her sister that she'd barely stopped to wonder just why Zayed had been so insistent about taking her out for dinner. No doubt she would find out soon enough. Opening up her wardrobe, she cast an uninterested eye over its contents but clothes had never been important to her and, anyway, she doubted the arch-seducer Sheikh would notice what someone like *her* was wearing. She gave a faint shudder of distaste as she thought about the Kafalahian ruler's reputation with women, before pulling on a warm sweater and thick tights to go with her tweed skirt—because the autumn evening had a decided nip to the air.

There was a knock at the door and Jane didn't miss the chauffeur's look of astonishment when she opened it, though—to the man's credit—he instantly tried to disguise it with a polite smile, especially when she greeted him in fluent Kafalahian. Looking glaringly out of place, the royal limousine was parked outside the small house owned by a college friend of hers, which had been divided into two apartments—the top one of which Jane rented. Still. At least her friend was working abroad and not around to witness the bizarre spectacle of a Kafalahian flag on the bonnet of the car, flapping in the light breeze.

It felt weird to have the driver open the door for her and for her to slide somewhat awkwardly onto the soft leather seat, because she'd never travelled in one of the royal cars before. There was a small fridge in situ, along with a glittering row of crystal glasses—as well as a TV screen much bigger than the one in her apartment. Jane stared out of the window at the darkening evening, wondering just what she was going to do about Cleo. Maybe she could ask Zayed for some sort of pay-rise. She bit her lip. It would have to be a fairly hefty pay-rise and she would need to have it immediately in order to bail her sister out.

'We're here, miss.'

The driver's voice broke into her troubled thoughts and Jane blinked. The journey had been so smooth that she hadn't even noticed the car gliding to a halt and suddenly the door was being opened again—this time by a uniformed porter, who was ushering her into an exclusive members' club, discreetly positioned in a wide street not far from Leicester Square Tube station. A mighty door clanged shut behind her as she stepped into an interior of pure opulence and grandeur—a cavernous hall lined with dark oak panelling and more paintings on the walls than you'd see in one of the nearby national art galleries. As Jane followed the porter inside, she became aware of several older women decked in dazzling jewels, who were peering at her as if she were a curiosity, with no right to be there.

In truth, she *did* feel more than a little out of place because even she, with her practically zero experience of social occasions, could tell that she'd woefully misjudged the occasion. There was nothing *wrong* with her knee-length tweed skirt or sweater, but they looked ridiculously understated in this grand and formal setting. And then another door was being flung open and there was Zayed, standing beside a carved marble fireplace, in which scented logs smouldered and crackled. He was wearing a flowing thawb in palest gold, which emphasised the burnished gleam of his skin and the raven blackness of his thick hair. Jane felt an unwelcome punch to her heart and the flicker of something warmer, low in her belly, as she met his flashing black eyes—though he did nothing to disguise the contemptuous curve of his lips as he stared at her.

'Is this some kind of joke?' he demanded.

She honestly didn't know what he was talking about—and she was still so preoccupied with Cleo's worries that she couldn't work it out. 'A joke, Your Royal Highness? I don't understand.'

'Really?'

His tone was imperious now, managing to be both haughty and condescending. She had never seen him pulling out all the royal stops before and Jane was suddenly reminded of why he was known as Zayed The Majestic in his homeland.

'Yes, really,' she said.

His eyes narrowed, throwing into relief his dark winged brows as his disbelieving gaze skated over her. 'I invited you for dinner,' he bit out. 'Told you to take the rest of the day off in readiness and yet you turn up to my club looking like some suburban housewife on the school run!'

Jane felt her cheeks flush with colour but she kept her gaze steady as she returned his. 'I don't have any fancy clothes or jewels,' she said stiffly.

'But you have a hairbrush, don't you? And a pretty dress? And surely it isn't outside the realms of possibility that you might have reddened your lips and darkened your eyes so that it might please me to look upon you.'

'I don't particularly want you to look upon me and I certainly don't care about pleasing you!' Jane retorted, before she had time to think about her words. And then she wished she could have bitten them back because she was planning on asking him a *favour*, wasn't she? Not making his face grow even darker with anger. She sucked in a breath and adopted a smile which felt as forced as the first Christmas dec-

orations which had started appearing in the stores at
the beginning of September. 'I… I'm sorry. I didn't
mean to sound rude.'

'No? Then I'd certainly hate to hear what you
might come out with if you were.'

He seemed to be making a conscious effort not
to lose his temper and very briefly Jane wondered
why—because Zayed was not a man known for his
patience.

'Why don't you try to relax and enjoy yourself?'
he continued condescendingly. 'And I shall get someone to bring you a glass of champagne.'

It was on the tip of her tongue to tell him she
didn't really drink champagne—apart from that
cheap fizz she'd had on the night of her eighteenth
and which had made her wake up with a splitting
headache. Why would she drink something associated with glamour? She wasn't Cleo. But she took a
foaming crystal goblet, which had been brought in on
a tray by a butler, who had appeared as if by magic.

'I have ordered food for us,' said Zayed airily.
'Since I do not wish to waste any more time than is
necessary with you fussing over the menu.'

'Shouldn't you have checked with me first to
check that I don't have any food allergies?' she said,
annoyed by yet another display of his presumption
and arrogance. 'Since I don't actually eat meat.'

'Well, isn't that a coincidence? Neither do I,' he

responded silkily, sitting down at the table, his powerful frame seeming to completely dwarf the gilt chair. 'At least that's one thing we *do* have in common. Sit, Jane.'

As she lowered herself stiffly into the chair opposite him, Zayed leaned back to study her a little more, still unable to believe just how drab she looked. He thought about his mistress in New York and how *she* might have appeared if she had been invited to dinner at his club—with her creamy breasts spilling out of one of those 'bandage' dresses she was so fond of, her slim legs encased in silk stockings and heels so high they should have carried a health warning.

But despite her bare face, her tied back hair and her appalling clothes sense, there was an intelligence about Jane Smith's eyes which was rare to behold. She had an undiscernible air of complexity about her—as if there were layers to this woman which he'd never encountered before.

He shook his head, reminding himself that her peculiarities were as inconsequential and as forgettable as a brief breeze which wafted through the high heat of summer. She was a means to an end and nothing more. He gestured for the main course to be carried in and nodded as it was placed in front of them, for he had decided against an appetiser. Why drag out this meal for longer than was necessary when all he needed to do was to get her to agree to his plan?

He waited for her to come out with some nicety. Maybe some shy little question about why he wanted to see her, but to his annoyance she didn't seem to be paying him any attention. Even her plate of food was barely touched as she peered over his shoulder and he had to turn round to discover that she was staring at a painting on the wall behind him and not at *him*.

'Is that the Kafalahian desert?' she questioned.

He nodded. 'Indeed it is. I donated it to the club,' he conceded reluctantly.

'I *thought* I recognised it. That's Tirabah in the distance, isn't it? You can just about see the three blue towers, if you look carefully.'

Zayed was torn between admiration for her obvious love of his country and irritation that she was effectively ignoring *him*. Because he wasn't used to being ignored. He ate a couple of mouthfuls of the spiced rice, pistachio and pomegranate dish—his favourite and one specially prepared for him whenever he came here—before laying down his fork. He noticed she wasn't eating, but that didn't surprise him. Women were often too awed to be able to consume food in his presence.

'Tell me about yourself, Jane Smith,' he said suddenly.

Jane put her fork down and looked up at him, grateful to be able to give up her pretence of eating. The food smelt delicious but she was still so churned up with anxiety for Cleo that it had ruined her appetite. She gazed at him suspiciously. 'Why do you want to know?'

'Because I do,' he answered unhelpfully.

She pursed her lips. 'Are you unhappy with my work?'

'No, Jane—but I am growing increasingly unhappy about your inability to answer a straight question.'

She stared at him, willing herself not to be mesmerised by the ebony gleam of his eyes but that was pretty much impossible. She wondered how it was that you could be repulsed and infuriated by a man and yet still your heart would pound like a piston whenever you looked at him.

'What do you want to know?'

'How you ended up working in my embassy and having an unrivalled knowledge about my country.'

Ignoring her champagne flute, Jane took a sip of water, slightly confused about where exactly to begin. Did she tell him that she'd been a quiet and serious child who used to lose herself in the world of books? That she'd been more like her academic father than the beautician mother who had been his surprising choice of wife?

No. Zayed Al Zawba wasn't interested in the personal. He wanted to know about her qualifications—and if she was planning to ask him for a pay-rise, or a loan, then wouldn't it be in her best interests to be honest about them for once, instead of playing down her achievements for fear that it might come over as boasting?

'I studied at the School of Oriental and Asian Studies in London and it was there that I became aware of some of Kafalah's great lyric poets. I became obsessed with one in particular and it was he who inspired me to learn your language so that I could translate his verses.' She smiled as she thought about the impact those poems had first had on her. The sudden realisation of just how powerful words could be. 'You will, of course, be familiar with the work of Mansur Beyhajhi?'

'I have no interest in poetry,' he said carelessly. 'That was more my father's line.'

Jane tried not to wince at his reaction but she wasn't sure if she managed it. But even though she was appalled at his cavalier dismissal of the greatest poet his country had ever produced, she shouldn't have been surprised. He hardly had a reputation as a man of great sensitivity, did he? He was known for racing fast cars and flying in private jets, as well as his legendary sexual consumption of beautiful women. And yes, everyone knew he was a wizard at playing the stockmarkets which added even more to the financial reserves of his oil-rich country—but that didn't stop Jane from sometimes thinking it was a pity that Kafalah had such a *barbarian* for a ruler. Had the early deaths of his parents contributed to his insensitivity—or had the responsibilities of having to rule at such a young age hammered them out of him?

Try to make allowances for him, she thought.

'Of course not,' she said. 'For a moment I quite forgot that you are a man of action, rather than a man of letters.'

There was a slow intake of breath from the other side of the table, a low hissing—not unlike how she imagined a striking snake might sound.

'You make me sound like an intellectual and cultural lightweight. Was that your intention, Miss Smith?'

'I thought we were supposed to be talking about me, Your Serene Highness, not you.'

His black eyes narrowed. 'And I note you've neatly avoided answering my question.'

Jane nodded. *Keep him sweet,* she urged herself. *Whatever it takes, just keep him sweet*. 'You are a desert sheikh whose role is to work for his country,' she said boldly. 'It is not necessary for you to love poetry.'

He gave a brief nod, as if partially mollified by her diplomatic reply. 'Go on,' he said. 'Tell me about yourself.'

She drew in a deep breath. 'I wrote an essay about Beyhajhi which caused some excitement in the aca-

demic world and I was called to your embassy by the
then Ambassador, who wanted to speak to me about it.
He offered me a job right there and then—cataloguing,
translating and preserving the beautiful manuscripts
which your father had collected and rescued from the
country during his life. To be honest...' And for the
first time that day, Jane properly relaxed as she remembered how that job offer had felt. As if everything had
slotted into place. As if for the first time in her life, she
was exactly where she was supposed to be. 'It was my
dream job,' she admitted, with a smile. 'And I leapt at
the chance.'

Zayed stilled, momentarily taken aback by the
impact of that unexpected smile. Why, it made her
face light up as if it had been illuminated by sunshine. For the very first time he noticed that her eyes
were the colour of caramel and that her enthusiasm
had made them gleam, like the most precious amber.
Why the hell didn't she smile like that more often,
instead of walking around with such an uptight and
prissy expression?

But she *was* prissy, he reminded himself—and
that was exactly why she was perfect for the role he
had in mind. He didn't want an attractive woman
who flashed her eyes and her body at him, who might
tempt him into sex. He wanted a brief, businesslike
marriage in order to attain Dahabi Makaan for his

people—and then a swift termination of their non-consummated union.

'You love my country, don't you?' he questioned suddenly.

'Absolutely,' she said simply.

'Yet you have never visited it before?'

'No. I haven't.'

She attempted another smile but this time it was more of a grimace, he noted.

'But you would like to?'

She looked at him with the expression of a child on a boiling hot day who had just been asked whether they would like an ice cream. 'Of course I would. But I can't just *go*. I would need to be invited. I'd need to have somewhere to stay. And anyway,' she added, her face crumpling as if she'd just remembered something, 'I can't afford it.'

'But if you *were* invited,' he said slowly, 'and if money were no object, you would go.'

A trace of impatience entered her intelligent eyes. 'Obviously.'

'Than I think we can be of service to one another.'

She frowned. 'I'm getting increasingly confused, Your Royal Highness. You invited me out for dinner and I'm still not sure why. Won't you tell me what your purpose was for asking me here tonight?'

He nodded, reminding himself that he needed to be stern and to lay down all the guidelines right from the beginning. She needed to be made aware of the honour he was about to bestow on her. 'I need a wife,' he said simply. 'And you are the perfect candidate.'

CHAPTER THREE

JANE STARED ACROSS the candlelit table in astonishment, for a moment thinking she might have misheard him, but the expression on the Sheikh's face told her it was no mistake. Through the flicker of the candle's flames his mouth was unsmiling and his black eyes were flat and unwavering as they fixed her in their gaze. She found herself thinking that if it wasn't a mistake then maybe it was some elaborate kind of joke which nobody had bothered to tell her about. A man like Zayed proposing marriage? To *her*?

'How can I *possibly* be the perfect candidate to be your wife?' she questioned defensively, as it occurred to her that he might be making fun of her. 'When everyone knows you've dated some of the most beautiful women in the world and I am nothing but one of your lowly outreach employees!'

'You are a most valued employee,' he said carefully.

'But an employee all the same—not one of your many girlfriends!' She glared at him. 'What kind of mischief is this you make with your words, Your Royal Highness?'

He looked taken aback by her accusation and that pleased her—it made her feel as if she was in possession of at least *some* control in a life which was currently very short of it. Her nerves were already shot with worry about Cleo, without the added headache of having to work out what sort of game the arrogant Sheikh was playing with his verbal riddles.

'It is not mischief,' he said slowly, 'but a genuine need to find myself a wife as quickly as possible.'

'But I'm not—'

'Yes, I know,' he put in impatiently. 'You fulfil none of the criteria which would naturally be expected of my bride. You are not royal, nor rich, nor beautiful—'

Her heart contracted. 'Is this some sort of character assassination?'

'No,' he said simply. 'It is the truth. And the very qualities which make you unsuitable—also make you the perfect candidate to be my bride.'

'You're still not making any sense,' she said.

'Then let me spell it out for you as simply as I can.' He leaned back, thoroughly at home in the sumptuous private room of his members' club. 'You

are aware of the recent death of my maternal grandfather?'

'Yes. My condolences to Your Royal Highness
for his loss.'

He inclined his head. 'In his will, he bequeathed
me a piece of land—'

'Which piece of land?' she interrupted curiously.

'Dahabi Makaan.'

She nodded, pursing her lips together to make a
silent whistle. 'Wow,' she said softly. 'That is a sig-
nificant bequest. Not only oil rich, but of consider-
able strategic importance in the desert region.'

His eyes narrowed with something like admiration. 'Forgive me for overlooking your comprehensive knowledge of the area.'

'Please carry on,' she said coolly, forcing herself
not to react to the compliment.

He looked into her eyes. 'It is, as you say, of con-
siderable strategic importance. A surprising gift
from a man from whom I had been estranged for
many years.'

'I knew there was some sort of rift,' she said cautiously, 'which was never really documented, although many historians note that the two families
were ruptured when your mother married your father.'

'The reasons are irrelevant,' he clipped out. 'All
you need to know is that the rift was healed when I

visited him on his deathbed. When all the angers and divisions which life can create count for nothing. He reached out and held my hand and it was strange to see how age had diminished him. I could see regret on his features—more regret, perhaps, than is usual just before the moment of death.'

His throat constricted and for the first time Jane thought she saw emotion on his face—a dark and bitter look which made his features appear almost *savage*, until he appeared to recover himself and the arrogant mask slipped back into place.

'As he gripped my fingers,' he continued, 'he looked into my eyes and told me he had been watching my sheikhdom from a distance and that he approved of the way I ruled my people. I told him that I was not seeking his approval, that he was not in a position to offer it, since he had rejected his only daughter when she chose to marry my father—and that had broken her heart.'

'What did he say?' questioned Jane breathlessly, for the dying king had been a formidable presence in the desert world.

'He laughed,' said Zayed. 'And told me I was strong but reckless.'

'And was he right?'

'Of course he was. My strength is legendary.' His ebony gaze mocked her. 'And I *like* being reckless.'

And something whispered down Jane's spine

when he said that. Something she'd never actually experienced before but which was instantly recognisable, because she'd studied enough of the erotic and very explicit literature of his country to recognise desire when she felt it. Inappropriate desire which would never be reciprocated. *Desire for the desert king.* It whispered over her skin with silken fingers. It spread through her veins like warm honey. Beneath the thickness of her sweater, she could feel her breasts begin to prickle.

Her lips suddenly felt dry and hot and she licked them. 'I still don't see where any of this is going. You healed your rift with the King and he bequeathed you a valuable piece of land. I should imagine that must give you cause for much rejoicing, instead of being here when you'd clearly much rather be somewhere else.'

He nodded as if to acknowledge the accuracy of her words before his expression suddenly grew serious.

'It's not that simple,' he said softly. 'Because, unfortunately, the bequest comes with a condition—which is that I must be married in order to inherit. And although the very idea is abhorrent to me, I want that piece of land for my people,' he said, his voice growing deep with fervour. 'So much so, that I'm prepared to marry in order to get it.'

'Then why not ask one of your many girlfriends?'

she questioned archly. 'Why not ask the mistress it is rumoured you keep in a luxury apartment in Manhattan?'

'Because she is in love with me,' he said simply. 'As most women I date inevitably are. And I cannot marry a woman who is in love with me because love makes women unreasonable. It makes them start longing for things they can never have.'

She frowned. 'I don't understand.'

'Because I don't want love and I don't wish to be tied to one woman—at least not until I have reached the age when my hair has grown silver and it is time for me to produce an heir. The union I propose with you will be nothing other than a means to an end. A brief union which I intend to be dissolved after six months.'

She looked at him curiously. 'On what grounds?'

'Non-consummation, of course.' He shrugged his powerful shoulders. 'I will not be having sex with my new bride.'

Jane nodded, her heart pounding painfully against her ribcage, her mind working over the facts as she pieced together the intention behind his bizarre request. 'So you decided to pick a woman to whom you were not in the least bit attracted?'

'Exactly.' He leaned back in his chair, his black eyes lasering into her.

'And I am that woman.'

'You most certainly are. I cannot think of a more ideal candidate.'

'I see.' Jane could hardly get the words out she was breathing so heavily. She wanted to shout at him. To ask what right he had to insult her like that. To do something utterly uncharacteristic like picking up her plate and tipping the rainbow rice all over his arrogant head, before storming out of the club with a veiled suggestion about what he might like to do with his offer. Until she reminded herself that she was in no position to do any such thing. Why risk losing the job she loved just because her pride had been hurt?

Because Zayed needed her, she realised.

And maybe she needed him.

Why rail against him for merely stating the truth? She knew her limitations and she'd never been the kind of woman who men hit on. She didn't dress to attract. She didn't pore over fashion magazines or experiment with make-up. She'd always relied on her mind and never bothered about her appearance—she'd left that to her mother and Cleo.

Cleo.

Jane's heart contracted painfully. Cleo, who owed so much money that men with threatening voices had started making sinister phone calls to *her*. Had she forgotten about that? Forgotten the fear which had fizzed through her veins when she'd spoken to her sister earlier that day and heard her on the brink of fearful tears? She had agreed to this unexpected dinner with Zayed partly because she'd been planning to ask him for a loan, or maybe a pay-rise—but perhaps his outrageous proposition had put her in a much more advantageous position than that. A powerful bargaining position. He wanted her hand in marriage—so why not ask him for something in return?

'You think I could bear to be married to a man like you for six months?' she questioned, trying to keep her voice steady.

'I think you could bear it very well. For a start you would get to visit Kafalah,' he said, his seductive tone mimicking that of a hypnotist who was dangling a swinging object before his goggle-eyed subject. 'Why, you'd even get to stay in the famous royal palace.'

His insolent words took Jane's breath away. So he was manipulative, as well as arrogant! Did he really think she'd be content to endure months of his unbearable company in order to see first-hand some of the antiquities she'd spent most of her adult life studying?

No. Sheikh Zayed Al Zawba was going to have to pay a much higher price than unlimited access to the treasures of Kafalah. She stared down at the pristine white linen napkin which lay neatly over her tweed skirt, aware of needing to choose her words carefully, because once said they could not be taken back. It would be wonderfully satisfying to refuse him outright. To look down her nose at him and tell him that his suggestion was inappropriate and insulting and she could think of no worse fate than being stuck with him for half a year. But she couldn't afford to turn his offer down. Not if the price were right. It would mean having to tolerate the company of a man who made her hackles rise, even while he managed to make her body ache in places it had never ached before. His presence was infuriating, intoxicating and yet ultimately danger-ous to her sense of worth. She suspected that peace of mind would not come easily if she became his bride, yet—if she was being realistic—how much time would she actually have to spend with him, even if they *were* married?

She knew Kafalahian custom meant the monarch was all-powerful and that these royal marriages were not *modern* marriages. It wasn't as if they'd be shar-ing chores or doing the weekly shop together. Zayed would doubtless be having diplomatic meetings in the palace or charging round the countryside on one of his famous black stallions. They wouldn't be ex-pected to spend much time together—only to give the *appearance* of being married—leaving her free to explore the glorious palace and all its gems.

'If I were to agree,' she said, lifting her gaze from the napkin to find those black eyes trained unwaveringly on her, disconcertingly making her think of a bird of prey... She swallowed. 'I would expect some kind of recompense.'

'Recompense?' he echoed, a frown creasing his brow. 'You mean money?'

She heard the faint distaste in his voice, as if he'd just been reminded that everybody had their price, and a flush of guilt flooded to her cheeks until she forced herself to remember that he wasn't her *friend*. She didn't owe him anything and she certainly didn't need his approval. He was quite prepared to exploit her love for his country to get her to consent to marry him—so why not exploit his grossly inflated bank account in order to save her sister's skin? Only rich people, she thought grimly, could be so dismissive of other people's worries about money.

'Of course I mean money,' she said. 'Don't you think I should be rewarded for having to enter into such a union as this?'

He glowered. 'You would obviously be given a settlement after the marriage has been annulled. Surely your greed could be tempered until then?'

'Not really. I need it now,' she said, more urgently than she'd intended.

'Oh?' He looked at her and his voice grew cold. 'And why is that?'

She opened her mouth to tell him, before thinking better of it. Zayed was reckless, yes, but he was also clever—and completely unscrupulous. They said that knowledge was power—something he already had more than his fair share of. Why reveal more about herself and her family than she needed to, when she had no idea how he might use that power?

'Oh, just personal reasons,' she said lightly. 'Which I won't burden you with. I'm sure it would bore you, Your Highness.'

A look of irritation crossed his face and Jane suspected he was one of those men who only wanted something when he was told he couldn't have it. *So start showing some strength. Put* him *on the back foot.*

'So,' she said. 'Do we have a deal, or have you changed your mind?'

'How much?' he demanded.

Quickly doing sums in her head, Jane gave him the amount which Cleo had mentioned and added a reasonable sum for interest—but his face gave barely a flicker of reaction as he nodded his head in agreement.

'Satisfied now?' he questioned archly.

'Not quite. There's just one other condition which needs clarification before I agree to become your wife.'

'More conditions?' he snapped. 'You drive a hard

bargain, Jane Smith. Hurry up and tell me, because my patience is wearing thin.'

This bit was much more difficult but Jane was determined to go through with it because—although she intended making a sacrifice for her sister—she would not be made a fool of.

'You say you wish the marriage to be dissolved within six months on the grounds of non-consummation.'

'I don't imagine that's going to be a problem for either of us, do you?' he questioned pleasantly.

She found herself thinking that even when he was trying to be agreeable, he still managed to be insulting. 'Not for me,' she admitted, hoping she was managing to convey the fact that he repulsed her, rather than the more disturbing revelation that she was still a virgin. 'But rather more so for you, I imagine—since you don't strike me as the kind of man who would choose to embrace a self-imposed period of celibacy.'

'You are a very perceptive woman,' he said silkily. 'For it is true that I cannot live without sex. But you strike me as intelligent enough to understand my appetites—even if you do not share them—and to discreetly look the other way.'

The near smirk which accompanied this remark gave Jane all the confirmation she needed and, although inwardly she was fuming, she hid her feelings beneath an air of composure.

'I will only agree to this if you vow not to sleep with other women.'

'Not to sleep with other women,' he repeated, as if she had just asked him to scale the north face of the Eiger without any climbing equipment.

'That's right.'

'You're jealous?' he questioned in surprise.

'Not at all. But I refuse to be made a fool of and there will be no deal unless you agree to cut all contact with your American mistress or, indeed, any other mistress, until after we are divorced. I don't want people laughing at me behind my back.'

Frustration vied with admiration in his jet-dark eyes as he shook his head slightly. 'You drive a hard bargain, Miss Smith.'

'Did you expect me to simply agree to everything you suggested?'

'Yes,' he said. 'I did.'

His candour momentarily disarmed her, enough to make her ask an unnecessary question—even though afterwards she would wish she hadn't bothered.

'And what would you have done if I'd had a boyfriend?' she asked. 'If I'd been unable to marry you at such short notice?'

His slow smile was more revealing than any words could have been, but that didn't stop him from say-

ing them. 'I would have talked you into it anyway,'
he boasted softly. 'Though I was fairly certain you
didn't have a boyfriend.'

Don't ask it.

She asked it.

'Oh? Why's that?'

He looked at her assessingly—the way she'd seen
farmers look in country markets when they were siz-
ing up how much to offer for a cow. And even though
it was a cold and calculating look, that didn't seem to
deter her body from reacting to it. There was a brief
tingle in her breasts as his gaze skated over them
and a heavy pulse started beating at her groin. For
a moment she felt helpless. Weak and vulnerable—
and yet it was a gorgeous feeling. As if she were
drowning in his gleaming black eyes yet wanting
to go even deeper. She wondered if he realised the
effect he was having on her—as if she were some
tightly closed flower bud slowly unfurling its petals
beneath the warmth of his scrutiny. As if the world
would suddenly feel like a very different place if he
pulled her into his arms and crushed her hard against
his muscular chest. And didn't she suddenly wish she
could wave a magic wand just to have one brief and
tiny taste of it? To test-drive her body to see whether
there were any traces of the sensuality which other
women of her age took for granted.

But she clamped down on her wistful feelings,

reminding herself that while Cleo's dreams had always been outsized, she'd kept her own modest and achievable. She knew her limitations, and Zayed must never become aware of the way he made her feel—that much was vital. She wasn't quite sure why—she just knew it was dangerous. Keeping her expression prim, she met his mocking gaze as she prepared to hear his answer, which instinct told her she wasn't going to like.

'Why am I so sure you don't have a boyfriend?' he drawled. 'Because you have an uptightness about you which is unusual. Both in your manner and in the way you dress. You don't strike me as a woman who is particularly *satisfied*.'

His black eyes gleamed with mischief and something else. Something which whispered over her skin with another warm lick of danger.

'In fact,' he continued softly, 'it wouldn't surprise me one bit to discover you were a virgin.'

CHAPTER FOUR

SHE SHOULD HAVE been excited.

Down below, where the tiny shadowed version of their plane was making its own parallel journey, lay the stark magnificence of the Kafalahian desert with its endless ripples of golden sand punctuated by the occasional crop of palm trees. Soon they would reach the ancient city of Tirabah, which housed the Sheikh's famous palace and which Jane had wanted to see ever since she'd first gone to college. Going to Kafalah had been a dream she'd never thought she'd realise so, yes, she should have been very excited. But she wasn't.

She was scared.

Scared of what lay ahead. Of blindly having agreed to marry someone who was everything she despised in a man. Of being in such close proximity to Zayed Al Zawba and at the mercy of the unexpected feelings which flooded over her whenever he looked at her.

She told herself she'd had no choice. Because hadn't accepting the Sheikh's proposal meant she'd been able to give her sister the money she needed, having first extracted the promise that she would start living within her means? She had batted off Cleo's questions about how she'd obtained the money but her twin's face had been unforgettable when Jane had whispered the news she'd requested be kept quiet for the time being.

'You're marrying the Sheikh of Kafalah?' Cleo's voice had been incredulous. *'You?'*

'That's right.'

'You mean the hot Sheikh who's always in the papers?'

'Some people think he's hot.'

'Presumably you do, too—if you're about to become his wife.'

But when Jane hadn't answered, Cleo's emerald eyes had widened—eyes so unlike Jane's and not only in colour, shaded as they were with layers of smoky grey shadow, their spiky lashes lengthened and darkened by several coats of mascara.

'You're doing it for me, aren't you? That's where you got the money from—by marrying a known philanderer who can't keep it in his trousers?' Cleo had bit her lip. 'Jane, I can't let you.'

'But you can't stop me and I won't even let you try. Because what else can I do?' Jane had sounded fierce but then she had forced a crooked kind of smile. 'Honestly. It isn't such a hardship.'

Had she really said that? Said that and meant it? In which case, why hadn't she been able to get a decent night's sleep since Zayed had flown back to his country ahead of her, in order to prepare for their wedding? Why had she started waking up when the world was still dark, her nightdress damp with perspiration and an insistent aching between her legs?

'We are just coming in to land, Miss Smith.'

Startled from her reverie, Jane looked up to see the stewardess smiling at her and she wondered how Zayed's staff were going to react when they discovered he had chosen such a mouse as his bride.

'Thank you,' she replied in Kafalahian, unable to deny the pleasure she got from witnessing people's surprise at her fluency in a language which few Westerners spoke.

The stewardess smiled and inclined her head before replying in the same language. 'You are most welcome. The Sheikh's assistant has just radioed ahead to say that His Royal Highness has arrived at the airport to greet you and the pilot estimates we will be landing in ten minutes, if you would like to freshen up.'

Jane nodded and, once the stewardess had gone, made her way to one of the two luxury bathrooms which were situated at the back of the aircraft, run-

ning her wrists under the cold tap and splashing
her face with water. But her cheeks still felt hot and
sticky when she emerged into the bright sunlight of
the Kafalahian day to see a long black car waiting
on the tarmac and beside it the unmistakable form
of Zayed Al Zawba.

His robes were of purest white, which reflected
the brilliant light, and for once his head was covered as he dominated the stark outline of the desert
landscape behind him. Her own linen trousers and
the matching top, which she'd chosen for practical-
ity and coolness, were now slightly crumpled after
the long flight and Jane knew she wasn't imagining
the contemptuous curve of his lips as she walked towards him. She told herself it didn't matter what he
thought of her appearance. Actually, maybe it was
better this way. Better he looked at her with nothing
more than disdain because surely that would stop her
stupid body from reacting whenever he was near.

But her heart was doing that mad racing thing
again and her breasts were pushing insistently
against her top as his piercing black gaze raked over
her. She could feel unfamiliar heat arrowing towards
her groin as she struggled to sound completely calm,
but her words still came out as a breathless little
stutter.

'Hello, Your R-royal Highness,' she said.

For a moment Zayed didn't trust himself to answer. He wanted to demand why she had dared to arrive at his desert home looking like something the goat had dragged down from the mountain. Thank the stars she would soon be dressed by the palace servants as Kafalahian tradition dictated, and hopefully they might be able to fashion some kind of miracle to convince his people that she was a suitable bride. But they were going to have their work cut out, he conceded. Did she deliberately dress in such a lacklustre style—even when flying to the country of her royal groom just before their wedding? He suspected that she had no interest in clothes, but now was not the time to take her to task on it, for wasn't it in both their interests for her introduction to palace life to happen as smoothly as possible?

So he gave a curt nod as he opened the car door for her and slid on the seat next to her, noting automatically that she edged a little further away from him, pressing her knees primly together. If it hadn't been so insulting, it might have been amusing. Did she really think she was in danger of him making a pass at her? Did she really imagine he'd want to run his fingertips over crumpled linen when he was used to women clothing themselves in satins and silks? Or that he was turned on by the way she'd scraped all her hair back into that tight and unforgiving bun? 'You're going to have to stop addressing me so formally,' he said, as the car pulled away. 'And get used to calling me Zayed.'

'Yes. I suppose I am.'

'So say it. Say my name to me.'

He could see her lips tighten as if she objected to being issued with such an order.

'Zayed,' she said.

He felt his pulse quicken, because wasn't such veiled insurrection almost *exciting*? 'Now say it again,' he instructed. 'Say it softly, in a way which could convince a visiting member of state that you are soon to be my adoring wife.'

He saw her hands tighten into fists. 'Zayed,' she repeated, digging out the word as if it were an unwanted weed.

'Slightly better,' he conceded. 'But it's going to require a lot of work.'

She was staring out of the tinted windows, as if she was drinking in the sight of the passing desert landscape, but her face was pensive as she turned back to look at him.

'It's still proving a difficult concept to get my head around—that I'm actually going to be your wife,' she admitted.

'I imagine the payment you're getting will help you get used to it.' There was a pause. 'What did you do with the money I gave you?'

She raised her eyebrows. 'Is that really relevant?'

'I thought husbands were supposed to know everything about their wives—every thought which flits through their heads. Isn't that the modern way of marriage?'

'But you are to be my husband in name only and for a limited tenure. None of this is real, is it?'

He shrugged. 'I don't imagine that you are used to dealing with such large sums. If you like, I can get one of my financial advisors to speak to you about investment. You might want to think about getting yourself some property.'

'Are you aware just how patronising that sounds?' she hissed, sounding as if she was struggling to control her breathing. 'I won't be making any investments. The money is for my sister.'

'Why?'

She shrugged and suddenly he stopped noticing her ugly top because his attention was drawn to the slight quiver of the breasts beneath. 'She was in debt,' she said baldly.

'Lucky sister to have someone who's prepared to endure six months with a difficult man, in order to come to her rescue,' he said softly.

'That's what families do,' she said. 'They stick together.'

Not his, he thought bitterly. His had been destroyed before he'd had a chance to get to know them properly.

Forcing himself to push his distracting thoughts away, he realised that it shouldn't have surprised him to realise she was helping out her sister. The idea that she'd been dazzled by the lure of instant wealth had never really fitted with what little he knew of her.

Sitting next to her like this, he found it easy to disregard her crumpled clothes and notice instead how clear her skin was and how brightly her eyes shone. A sign of clean living? he wondered. Probably. He thought she seemed *overlooked*—like a book which had been pushed to the back of a shelf and nobody had ever bothered to study properly. Perhaps she was comfortable with that. Perhaps that was why she dressed in such a drab way, in order to fade into the background and remain unnoticed. Yet her dedicated work ethic certainly made her stand out and her sometimes stern and forthright attitude was something he'd never encountered before—certainly not from any other woman who wasn't middle-aged, or a governess. The embassy staff had informed him how late she worked most nights—preferring to be deep in a pile of ancient manuscripts rather than going out on the town. What a mystery she was!

He thought about the taunt he'd made to her in London—the taunt she had deliberately refused to rise to, although a series of conflicting emotions had crossed over her features before she'd cut them off with that prim look he was already becoming familiar with. Could she *really* be a virgin? he wondered idly, his mouth drying as he felt lust harden his groin beneath the silk of his robes, because the lure of the unknown was potent to a man whose sexual appetite was sometimes jaded. He had enjoyed many women throughout a sensual career more comprehensive than most men his age, but he'd never had a virgin before. He had never experienced the sound of a woman's cry as he broke through her hymen, nor eased himself inside the fabled tightness. Even the women brought to him in his late teens to instruct him in the art of love had been chosen for their experience and expertise.

His mouth twisted as he remembered how his peers at university had openly envied the life he'd lived as a pampered royal, growing up in a lavish palace in a country he would one day rule. They knew he'd been given untold wealth and limitless freedom for most of his life, but they had not known the reason why. Why so many supposed gifts had been heaped onto his young head—as if women and gold and the finest stallions in the land could compensate for what had been ripped away from him, or for the guilt which had become his lifelong companion as a result.

He felt pain grip at his heart but he pushed it away with a ruthlessness born of many years' practice.

'You know what to expect?' he questioned suddenly. 'From the wedding ceremony itself and what happens afterwards?'

She nodded. 'It is my job to know and I have studied the protocol. I know that I'm to be dressed in the traditional Kafalahian gown worn only by royal brides—and that in my hair I will wear the ancient emerald crown of the Al Zawba dynasty.'

'That is exactly so. And you will also know that we shall be spending our wedding night together in a suite which has been specially prepared for the newlyweds, in the eastern tower of the palace. And that our waking moments are intended to witness the rising of the sun, symbolising the dawn of our new life together?'

'Yes.' Jane kept her voice low. She reached down to pick up her handbag from the floor of the car as a distraction exercise—momentarily too daunted to dare look him in the face, scared of what he might read in her eyes. Because he'd just highlighted the bit which was terrifying her. The part of the whole farcical wedding process which was making her stomach do peculiar flips. *Obviously*, they wouldn't be carrying out the ancient Kafalahian tradition which involved a bloodied sheet being dangled from a window to prove the bride's virginal status. Things had moved on since then, thank heavens. But they *would* have to spend the night together—and that was something she was dreading more with each second that passed.

She lifted her gaze to find Zayed's black gaze trained on her in that bird of prey thing he did so effortlessly and she tried not to shiver. Was he aware that just being close to him in a car was making her body react in a way which seemed beyond her control? That her pulse was racing and there was a warmth between her thighs which was highly distracting? And, if that was the case, how difficult was it going to be if she was closeted in a room with him on their fake wedding night?

So confront it. He hadn't held back from telling *her* the brutal truth, had he?

'But I don't suppose anyone will really care if we have separate rooms, will they?'

His eyes gleamed. 'On the contrary,' he said silkily. 'Tradition remains an important bedrock of Kafalahian life and I intend to honour that. This marriage is going to follow every rule in the damned book. Because even though I am only doing it in order to inherit, I might as well reap any other benefits it produces as a result. And it will please my people to think that their king has found himself a permanent woman at long last.'

'Even if it isn't true?'

'Even if it isn't true,' he echoed.

She twisted the strap of her handbag around her

fingers, aware of how cheap the fake leather looked
in contrast to the luxury which surrounded her.
'And won't your people be disappointed—saddened,
even—when you throw the towel in on the marriage
after six short months and say it isn't working?'

He shook his head. 'Not at all. I will simply issue
a statement saying I found it impossible to be married to a Westerner—that our cultures were too different—and I shall not marry again unless it is to a
Kafalahian woman. That will be enough to pacify
and to satisfy them. It will also keep a generation of
women amused and eager to see who I shall eventually pick as my permanent bride.'

Even though she told herself she was stupid to
care, Jane couldn't deny being hurt by his words.
What callous disregard he had for her! He seemed
to regard her like an object without any real feelings,
who could be moved around at will.

Peering out of the window again, she saw a building looming in the distance and suddenly her troubles were forgotten as she leaned forward to get a
better look at the famous palace of Kafalah. Her
heart began to pound with excitement. She was familiar with the iconic building since it featured on
just about every feature you ever read about Kafalah
or saw on TV, as well as in the thousands of paintings
and photos she'd seen during her years of working
at the embassy. But nothing could have prepared her

for that first dazzling sight as it rose up like a citadel from out of the desert landscape.

Covered in rose-gold leaf, its azure domes and turrets soaring into the cloudless sky, it glittered on the horizon like a costly treasure. A group of guards stood sentry outside massive gates scrolled with embellishments in silver and gold—and she knew that the inlaid diamonds which winked in the sunlight were real. A wide straight path, lined with tall palm trees, was flanked on either side by an ornate fountain—one symbolising day and the other night. Jane knew that within the sweeping grounds was a secret garden with a 'moon' mirror, positioned so that it could exactly frame the moon at its fullest and a place rumoured to be one of the most romantic on earth. She could see a flash of colour as the gates opened to allow their car through and she realised that late roses were blooming in a cultivated riot of crimson and apricot blooms. Ignoring the cool of the air-conditioning, Jane hit the electric window button and a waft of their deep and heady scent entered the car. It was everything she had ever thought and dreamed it could be and a deep breath of admiration rushed from her lips as they came to a halt in front of the huge arched doors, inlaid with opals which gleamed like rainbows.

'Oh, wow,' she said softly. 'I can't believe I'm actually here.'

'You like my home I think, Jane Smith?'

She'd almost forgotten he was there and Jane turned to find Zayed looking at her, his expression intense and somehow approving, and she wished he wouldn't *do* that. Why make his voice go all soft and caressing, so that each word was brushed over her skin like velvet? And why make his eyes gleam as if she'd just said something wonderful, instead of stating the very obvious—which was that the place where he lived was the stuff of fairy tales to most normal folk.

'I'm sure you don't need me to tell you that the rose-gold palace is a place of beauty,' she said stiffly, but her attempt to try to put the atmosphere on a more normal footing seemed to have horribly back-fired. Because instead of his coming back at her with a flippant response and displaying enough of his usual arrogance to remind her of just why she couldn't *stand* him—his black eyes were gleaming with something which looked like curiosity.

'What made you such a fierce woman?' he questioned quietly.

'I'm only fierce with certain people.'

'Like me?'

'Like you,' she conceded.

'And why is that?'

And all the answers she *could* have given suddenly failed to compute. His proximity was so distracting that she forgot all about the way she'd had to toughen up and grow an extra skin, in order to make everyone else's life easier. Suddenly, her reasons for being fierce in *these* circumstances became the ones she was trying not to think about. Like how sensual his lips looked and what it would be like to be kissed by them. And how his muscular body was making her picture all the erotic texts she'd been studying last week. Suddenly she felt fragile. As if one breath of his would be strong enough to make her topple over...straight into his arms.

Glaring at him, she clutched the strap of her handbag even tighter. 'You don't want to know why,' she said. 'My personality is completely irrelevant.'

'Oh, but I do,' he demurred silkily. 'And what is more, I intend to find out. How else are we going to pass the time?'

She didn't answer. She didn't dare. All she could do was turn her head to stare fixedly out of the window because it was easier than looking into the flashing black temptation of the Sheikh's eyes.

CHAPTER FIVE

At first Zayed thought he must be seeing things.

As the harp-like music of the *chang* heralded the bride's entrance he could do nothing but stare in disbelief. For a moment he thought that someone must have put an imposter in her place—for surely this could not be *Jane* walking towards him with her glittering crown of emeralds, clutching a bouquet of fragrant roses which had been gathered from the palace gardens soon after dawn?

Her jewel-encrusted wedding dress was modest in design for it covered every inch of her body, yet since ancient times the traditional royal bridal gown had been intended to showcase the female form in all its glory and to tempt the King who would be leading her to his bedchamber later that evening. He swallowed. And it did. By the bright moon in the heavens, it did.

Clinging like melted butter to the curve of her breasts, it emphasised a surprisingly tiny waist be-

fore falling in heavy swathes from the bell-like shape
of her hips. He felt the instinctive hardening of his
body in response. The heated rush of blood to his
groin. Who would ever have guessed that Jane Smith
possessed such a dynamite body beneath the drab
and shapeless outfits she normally favoured?

His eyes narrowed against the dazzling light of
the throne room because her physical transformation
didn't stop with her clothes. Sweet moon in the heavens, no, it did not. Zayed felt as if he'd been trying to
read a book with the curtains closed—only to pull
aside those drapes to find the words revealed with
startling clarity. He realised he'd only ever seen her
with her hair caught up in a tight bun and not wearing any make-up. But today…

Today…

Her amber eyes had been darkened with kohl
pencil so they looked moody and sensual and about
three times their normal size. Her lips were stained
a deep berry-red and as he stared at them he wondered why he'd never noticed those sensual cushions
before. Was not such a mouth designed to have a man
cover it with kisses—before putting it to work over
an erect and aching shaft to lick him to fulfilment?
And as for her hair… He shook his head slightly, because running his fingers through the hair of a fertile
woman was surely one of the most abundant pleasures
known to man and up until that moment he had been

unaware of Jane Smith's crowning glory. Instead of being constrained by an ugly bun, it tumbled down in a honeyed fall, caught back from her cheeks by two emerald clips, which helped secure the golden veil floating behind her like a diaphanous ray of sunshine.

The sharpness of the lust which rushed through him was all the more powerful because it was unexpected. He could feel it in the heat of his blood and the throb of his groin. And she was not looking at him...didn't that also fire up this sudden and inconvenient hunger? He was used to women looking at him with flirtation and desire sparking from their eyes, not for their heavy eyelids to be demurely lowered, shielding him from their expression and keeping him at a distance. As she reached him, those eyelids opened fractionally and once again he was struck by the beauty of her amber eyes, which today gleamed like darkest gold.

But beauty—like desire—was the most fleeting of life's gifts and Zayed's hunger was replaced by a twist of pain as she came to stand beside him. Because no matter how much you rationed painful memories, sometimes you couldn't prevent them from bombarding the mind, no matter how hard you tried. Wasn't it natural that he should remember his mother on a day like today? And wasn't it also natural for him to reflect bitterly that if she had not allowed herself to be swayed by the pernicious blend of hormones they called *love*, she might still be alive...

And he would not have to carry the burden of her death.

Guilt shafted through him but he was glad of its rapier-like plunge to his heart—because it helped clarify his thoughts and put things in perspective. Who cared if this was a bogus marriage? Not him. If his people secretly longed for the fairytale version of a royal wedding, then they were destined to be disappointed. Before the year was out they would need to accept that this marriage would be over— and it would be many years before he repeated such an unwanted exercise. His eyes were clear; his mind made up.

This was nothing but a means to an end.

As Jane reached his side he held out his hand for hers and noted the tremble of her fingers. Was she nervous? Or was she, like him, wondering how they were going to endure a night together—when the whole deal was that sex was off the menu? Until five minutes ago, he had barely given their impending night of chastity more than a fleeting thought— but suddenly he could sense a danger which simply had not occurred to him before.

What if his lust for her continued, or grew? What if this inconvenient desire demanded satisfaction?

His mouth flattened. He could not allow it to. No

matter how much—or how inexplicably—this former plain Jane tempted him, he could not have her.

'Okay?' he made himself ask as she reached him.

But if he had hoped for a little gratitude as she acknowledged his courtesy towards her, he was to be disappointed. Her expression was as fierce as ever as she looked up at him, her eyes silently telling him she'd rather be anywhere than here. And suddenly another powerful rush of adrenalin flooded through Zayed's veins—more potent than anything he had felt in a long time, because he wasn't used to getting the cold shoulder. He'd never had to fight for a woman, nor work to gain her affection. And he'd never really had to try in order to bed her. He felt another unwanted kick of lust as he met her stubborn expression. What he would give to be able to dismiss everyone in the room and to crush her lips beneath his in a mind-blowing kiss, before slipping his hand beneath the encrusted gown to encounter the cool flesh which lay there. That would have quickly wiped away her haughty expression!

'Zayed.'

Jane's voice broke into his erotic daydream and he realised she was now looking at him with the undeniable flicker of reproach in her eyes.

'What is it?' he demanded.

'Hassan was asking you a question and you were miles away,' she said.

What was he *thinking*? Was he really allowing forbidden fantasy to blind him to his duty? And why the hell was he fantasising about such an uptight woman as *this*? With an effort he turned to his aide. 'Yes, Hassan. What is it?'

'I was merely asking if you were ready to go through with the ceremony, Your Serene Highness.'

'Yes, yes,' said Zayed impatiently. 'Let's just get it over with.'

For Jane, the ceremony passed in a blur. She was aware of making vows in both Kafalahian and in English, and of Zayed slipping a ring onto her finger—a heavy golden ring studded with emeralds which matched those in her crown. She had studied the words beforehand in preparation, determined that she wouldn't stumble over any of them and grateful that her familiarity with Kafalahian would aid her fluency. She'd thought that learning the words by heart—as you did a list of verbs—would make them seem meaningless when she came to say them out loud. But it wasn't that easy. She could feel a little catch in her voice as she promised to love her Sheikh for ever with all her heart and body and soul. Suddenly she felt a hypocrite to be taking such solemn vows in vain and she prayed his people would not be disappointed by the inevitable outcome.

But what choice did she have if she wanted to free her sister from her past mistakes and give her a brand-new start? Hadn't Cleo promised faithfully that she would live within her means from now on—and even though Jane had felt doubtful if she'd be able to keep a promise when she'd broken so many in the past, she hadn't let it show on her face. And there were other benefits which would come about as a result of this strange union—she needed to remember those, too. Kafalah would be a much stronger and richer country as a result of Zayed inheriting Dahabi Makaan. Sometimes you had to make sacrifices for the greater good, she reminded herself. And surely it wouldn't kill her to play-act the part of the Sheikh's bride for half a year.

But there had been that moment right at the beginning which had made her heart miss a beat. The moment when she'd been walking towards him and seen him looking at her as if he couldn't quite believe his eyes—a look which probably matched her own reaction because she hardly recognised the Jane which had been reflected back at her when she'd stared at her wedding dress in the mirror. A sensual and subtly provocative Jane who seemed completely at odds with the inexperienced woman underneath all the bridal finery. But when Zayed's black gaze had roved disbelievingly from the tip of her emerald crown to the glimpse of the golden toe which peeped from beneath the weighted hem of her gown, she'd felt like a woman for the first time in her life. A woman who could appear almost lovely in the eyes of the beholder. A woman who could be *desired*.

But then she'd seen that look being replaced by another—an unfamiliar expression which had wiped away the habitual power and control and made his hawk-like features appear almost *ravaged*. Had that been pain or despair she'd seen in his night-dark eyes? Was the idea of being tied to her—even for so short a time—causing him such open distress? She chewed on her berry-stained lips. Well, that was just too bad. *He* was the one who had proposed this marriage of convenience which suited them both—and they were both going to have to make the best of it.

There was feasting after the ceremony, though not the three days of celebrations which some royal weddings in the region would have demanded. Zayed had opted to keep the event a decidedly low-key and local affair and Jane was grateful for that. Perhaps he realised it might be unwise to invite world leaders to witness a marriage which had the timer ticking on it from the outset. Which meant that although the claret and golden dining room was filled with guests and dignitaries, they were mainly royals from the desert region who would not gossip to the world media, nor try to take any forbidden 'selfies' when fireworks exploded over the palace lake. Karim of Maraban was there with his wife Rose, as well as the infamous prince who had once defied convention by marrying a humble stable girl.

Determined to emotionally distance herself from what was going on, Jane tried to view the whole affair through the eyes of an academic, reminding herself that she was taking part in a little bit of history. That one day she would merit a brief mention in textbooks—possibly even with a photo of her wedding day—before the inevitable footnote stating that the marriage had been dissolved a mere six months later.

But it was difficult to be *distant* when your body seemed to have developed a stubborn will of its own. When she found herself wanting to push her aching breasts against Zayed's powerful chest as he caught her in his arms for the traditional first dance between bride and groom. As it was, she could barely think straight and wasn't it the most infuriating thing in the world that he immediately seemed to pick up on that?

'You seem to be having trouble breathing, dear wife,' he murmured as he moved her to the centre of the marble dance floor.

'The dress is very tight.'

'I'd noticed.' He twirled her around, holding her back a little. 'It looks very well on you.'

She forced a tight smile but she didn't relax. 'Thank you.'

'Or maybe it is the excitement of having me this

close to you which is making you pant like a little kitten?'

'You're *annoying* me, rather than exciting me. And I do wish you'd stop trying to get underneath my skin.'

'Don't you like people getting underneath your skin, Jane?'

'No,' she said honestly. 'I don't.'

'Why not?'

She met the blaze of his ebony eyes and suppressed a shiver. 'Does everything have to have a reason?'

'In my experience, yes.' There was a pause. 'Has a man hurt you in the past?'

This was her chance to tell him yes—even though the very idea that someone had got that close to her was laughable. What difference would a lie make when they had already woven a complex web of deceit around themselves? But Jane had the disciplined mind of the academic and she knew it was pointless trying to fool someone unless you were qualified to do so—especially when you were dealing with someone as clever as Zayed. How could she possibly pretend to be a woman whose heart had been broken by a man, when she'd hardly even been kissed? There had been that ghastly encounter on the dance floor during her first term at uni, when a man had kept plunging his tongue into her mouth with the vigour of someone trying to unblock a toilet, and it had put her off for life. Zayed had already guessed she might be a virgin, but that didn't even come close to her shameful lack of experience.

Trying to ignore the way his groin was brushing against her as he edged her closer, she glanced up at him, her cheeks burning. 'I refuse to answer that on the grounds that I might incriminate myself. Tell me instead, do you always insist on interrogating women when you're dancing with them?'

'No. I don't,' he said simply. 'But then I've never had a bride before and I've never danced with a woman who was so determined not to give anything of herself away.'

'And that's the only reason you want to know,' she said quietly. 'Because you like a challenge.'

'All men like a challenge, Jane.' His black eyes gleamed. 'Haven't you learned that by now?'

She didn't answer—because how was she qualified to answer any questions about what men did or didn't like? She was grateful when the dance ended so she could escape the temptation of his touch—though, bizarrely, she found herself missing the feel of his body pressed close to hers. But her emotions were already in turmoil and she realised it wasn't going to get any better unless she took some sort of action. The trouble was that it was the wrong action. Her stomach was so churned up with the thought of the night ahead that she barely touched any of the wedding feast, but drank some of the sweet, herb-flavoured wine they called *karazib* instead, which immediately felt as if someone had injected fire into her veins. It was a warm and heady feeling, but she wasn't sure it was a wise one.

Was that the reason for her slight unsteadiness as she and Zayed made their way towards the eastern section of the palace, their process lit by a series of blazing torches—making her feel as if they were taking part in some medieval pageant? They climbed to the top of the eastern tower and, in spite of her nerves, Jane was blown away by the scene which greeted them. Scattered rose petals and dried lavender scented a path towards the four-poster bed, which was draped with embroidered hangings. The room was lit by tall candles and, outside the window, the full moon cast a silver path directly onto the bed.

'The palace staff have prepared the room for the bride and groom,' Zayed said softly.

The wooden door banged shut behind them and Jane's heart started hammering as she looked up at her new husband, unsure of what to do next. His shadow rose giant-sized on the wall behind him and he looked so dark and formidable as he stood in front of her that she honestly didn't have a clue where they went from here. If she'd never even kissed a man, it followed that she'd never shared a room with one before and even though the room was vast the walls seemed to be closing in on her. She started to wonder what she had let herself in for when she'd confidently agreed to his proposal in that London club, which now felt like a world away. Zayed had told her that there was to be no consummation but perhaps neither of them had taken into account the one glaringly obvious stumbling block to that.

She swallowed. 'There's only one bed.'

'But of course.' He pulled off his silken headdress and let it flutter down. 'It's a honeymoon suite.'

'I thought...'

'What did you think, Jane?'

Nervously, she looked around the room, searching for some kind of loophole. She read plenty of stories where men and women ended up stuck in the same bedroom—but wasn't there always a handy sofa or *chaise-longue* for one of them to spend the night on? Why, in here there wasn't so much as an armchair—and that narrow bench-like seat beneath the window didn't look wide enough to accommodate either of their frames.

'We're...not supposed to be having sex!' she said carefully.

'If you remember, I was the one who proposed celibacy within the marriage,' came his cool reply. 'You're preaching to the converted.'

'So what are we going to do?'

'About?'

'Sleeping. If we're forced to share the same bed?'

He shrugged. 'We lie side by side. We each allow ourselves to think how good it would be to touch one another in the most intimate way and we both reject the possibility, for obvious reasons. I lie there in a brief state of acute frustration before falling asleep— while you remain awake for hours, fretting, because that's what women tend to do.'

'You would know about that, of course.'

'Of course,' he allowed, with a slight incline of his raven head. 'For I have slept with many women.'

'And I suppose you're proud of that fact?'

'Of my ability as a lover, yes. Women enjoy my body—why wouldn't I take satisfaction in the knowledge that I bring them intense pleasure?'

Why not indeed? Yet his swaggering assurance made Jane want to lash out at him until she told herself that nothing would be accomplished by such impetuous behaviour. Why would she be remotely bothered about the behaviour of a man she despised? What did *she* care about the pleasure he brought to other women? They would simply have to do as he suggested and lie chastely, side by side. Thank heavens she had packed several baggy nightshirts and brought them with her from England.

When Zayed disappeared into the bathroom, she lifted one arm above her neck and bent it at the elbow as she attempted to lower her hand far enough to undo the tiny pearl buttons at the back of her dress, but it was far from easy. With a great deal of wriggling she managed three before her shoulder started aching and she was almost weeping with frustration as Zayed returned, wearing nothing but a very small white towel wrapped low over his hips. And suddenly all thoughts of getting undressed drained from her mind as the silver moonlight illuminated his muscular body.

'What…what do you think you're doing?' she demanded, her breath coming thick and fast.

'Getting ready to go to bed.'

She wanted to avert her gaze but it was impossible to look anywhere else other than at his magnificent body. At the broad, bare shoulders and powerful chest with the shadowed texture of dark hair, which contrasted against his gleaming olive skin. At the narrow hips and long, sturdy shafts of his muscular legs—and all the mysterious territory in between, which was covered by that insubstantial piece of white towelling. She swallowed. 'I hope you're not proposing to wear that in bed?' she demanded.

'What would you propose I wear?' he questioned.

Even to her own ears it was a preposterous suggestion but it was the only alternative she knew. 'Pyjamas.'

'Pyjamas.' His mouth twisted into the mockery of a smile as he repeated the word, making it sound as if he'd never actually used it before. 'A disgusting piece of apparel which I have never worn and never intend to. I'm planning on sleeping naked. I always do.'

'But you...'

'You?' He lifted his eyebrows enquiringly.

'Can't,' she said desperately.

'Why not?'

'You know why not!'

'Not unless you tell me, I don't.'

Angry with him for putting her through this, she supposed she could pretend—but how good was she at being blasé? She had no idea because it wasn't something she'd ever needed in her repertoire before now. And wasn't it a stretch too far to try to be someone she wasn't, given the already bizarre circumstances in which she found herself?

'I'm... I'm not used to men.'

'Explain,' he said, moving round to the back of her. 'And while you're explaining I'd better unfasten your dress so you don't have to look at me while you're telling me, trying desperately hard not to stare at my groin.'

'You're disgusting,' she snapped, trying to wriggle away from the fingers which were now brushing against her skin as he undid the fourth button.

'I'm a realist,' he demurred. 'And what else are you going to do if I don't help you undress? Sleep in your wedding dress?'

Jane bit her lip because he had a point. With its heavy embroidery and real gems, the full-skirted bridal gown weighed an absolute ton. It had felt as if she'd been carrying round bags of groceries all day and she was longing to be rid of it. 'Oh, very well,' she said crossly, feeling the delicious rush of cooling air on her skin as he freed another button.

'You were going to tell me,' he said as his fingers began to work their way skilfully down her back, 'why you weren't "used" to men.'

So did she tell him the truth? The unvarnished and somewhat painful truth? Maybe she should. It wasn't as if she was trying to *impress* him, was it?

'Because I was a bookish child.'

'Go on.'

She hesitated as his middle finger brushed over her skin, willing her stupid heart to quieten its frantic thumping. 'You know I'm a twin?'

'No. I just knew you had a sister. Is it relevant?'

'I think it probably is,' she said slowly, staring out of the palace window at the bright disc of the moon and thinking how surreal this all was. It was funny, really—because nobody had ever been remotely interested in hearing her story before, and even if they had been she would have quickly changed the subject to lose herself in the infinitely safer world of academia. But as he'd said himself, how else were they going to pass the time unless they talked—at least until they were tired enough to fall into the comforting arms of sleep?

'She is my non-identical twin,' she explained. 'And very lovely.'

'I see.'

He didn't say *But you are lovely, too*—which would have been the *polite* thing to do—and even though Jane supposed he should be commended for his honesty, that didn't stop it from hurting.

'So you were always classified as the clever one, while she was known as the beautiful one?' he continued thoughtfully. 'And the older you got, the more you grew into each of the roles to which you'd both been assigned?'

She almost turned round in surprise because she hadn't expected him to be quite so perceptive, until she remembered what he was wearing. Or rather, what he *wasn't* wearing. She carried on staring at the moon instead. 'How on earth did you know that?'

'It's a common enough pattern. We all grow into the roles which were given to us as children,' he said cryptically. 'I'm guessing your sister spent her teens trying to capitalise on her looks, while you concentrated on your studies?'

'You've been having me investigated,' she said crossly.

'No, I haven't.' He undid another button. 'You were security cleared when you first came to work at the embassy—that was enough for me. I'm merely tapping into a lifetime's habit of observing women, whose behaviour is far more predictable than you might imagine.'

'Well, if you're so clever, perhaps you can finish my story for me?'

There was silence as he undid another button and Jane briefly closed her eyes as she felt another tantalising brush of his fingers against her skin.

'I think you devoted pretty much all your time to study, with the single-mindedness which has made you such a hit at the embassy.'

'Careful, Zayed—that sounds awfully like a compliment.'

'And I imagine that sublimating your femininity was something which became a habit for you, because your pretty sister attracted all the attention. And that men were the last thing on your mind when you got a place at one of the best universities in the country.'

Jane swallowed. She wanted to damn him for his candid assessment even though the analytical side of her brain couldn't help but admire how accurately he had identified her personality type. 'Bravo,' she said. 'If ever you get bored with ruling your very own desert country, you could always try a career move into psychology.'

He gave a low laugh. 'Careful, Jane,' he warned

silkily. 'You may have rejected the very obvious methods of making yourself attractive to men, but I'm assuming nobody warned you about the sexual frisson produced by verbal sparring.'

Danger suddenly entered the air. A potent and powerful danger, which made Jane acutely aware of the cool evening air on her spinal column and the fact that all the buttons were now undone. She was half dressed in a bedroom with a near-naked sheikh standing right behind her—and wasn't there an unfamiliar part of her which wanted him to put his fingers right back where they had been? To start stroking her bare skin and slide the heavy dress down over her hips? Despite being freed from the tight corset, her breathing felt even more constricted and her voice was tight as she spoke. 'I'd like to get ready for bed now, if you don't mind.'

'Perhaps you'd like me to avert my eyes?'

Ignoring the sarcasm which coated his words, she nodded. 'Yes. That's exactly what I want.'

'Very well.' He walked over to the window and stared out at an indigo sky, which was spattered with stars. 'Feel free.'

Pulse racing, she hurried over to the wardrobe where the palace staff must have unpacked and hung up the clothes she'd brought with her but, despite her frantic search, she couldn't find her comforting nightshirts anywhere. The only garments which confronted her were several lace-trimmed satin night-gowns so delicate that when her fingers brushed against them, she was half afraid of tearing them.

'My nightshirts aren't here,' she said.

'You mean those hideous baggy T-shirts?'

'Where are they?'

'Gone, I imagine. And replaced with garments far more befitting for a queen.'

Indignantly she turned round to look at him then, and oh-so-predictably, the sight of his body spot-lighted by the moonlight completely jarred her equi-librium. The small white towel slung low at his hips seemed ridiculously small for the purpose for which it was intended. Because surely it was supposed to *conceal* the most secret part of his body instead of drawing attention to it so that she could hardly bear to drag her eyes away, just as he'd arrogantly stated.

'You had no right to throw away my things!'

'Nothing to do with me. Blame your ladies-in-waiting,' he retorted coolly. 'They probably thought it outrageous that the new Sheikha should be gracing her husband's bed clad in such unflattering attire.'

She directed her gaze to the floor, staring at the ground rather than the groin. 'Then what am I sup-posed to wear?'

'Once again you are testing my patience, Jane,' he said steadily. 'Just select one of the nightgowns specially flown in from Paris as part of your trousseau and wear one of those. Gratitude is optional, but would be much appreciated.'

Grabbing the first one on the rack, Jane didn't trust herself to answer as she scuttled into the bathroom and stepped out of her wedding dress and underwear before pulling the extravagant piece of lingerie over her head. Scrubbing the kohl make-up from her eyes and washing her face, she pulled the priceless emerald clips from her hair but an unexpected glimpse of herself in the mirror made her blink in disbelief. Because this was another unknown Jane. Not like the bride she'd been earlier—because that Jane had simply ticked a lot of necessary boxes and resembled pretty much any other royal Kafalahian bride down through the ages. But this Jane was different.

She swallowed.

Scarily different.

The kohl had gone but she'd been unable to shift the berry-red stain from her lips, which suddenly looked all pouty and trembling. Her loose hair tumbled freely over slippery satin and the material clung to her like a second skin—gleaming against the swell of breasts emphasised by a delicate edging of fine lace. She looked feminine but also…wanton. How could that be when Zayed hadn't laid a finger on her? But her eyes were unusually dark and two high lines of colour were slashed against her otherwise pale skin. And the nubs of her nipples were outlined clearly against her suddenly engorged breasts. Why, they looked almost twice their normal size.

How could she possibly go into their bedroom and face him when she looked like this—as if she were crying out for a man to have sex with her—while inside she felt vulnerable and scared and hopelessly out of her depth?

And then an image of Zayed's hawk-like features and near-naked body swam into her mind and suddenly her vulnerability drained away as an unfamiliar curiosity began to creep over her. What would happen if she returned to the bedroom and rubbed her body up against his, the way a cat sometimes did when it was winding its tail around someone's ankles? What if she pulled his dark head towards hers and demanded he kiss her? Would he?

That depended. She suspected that his will was as strong as iron, no matter how much she tried to tempt him—even if someone like her *could* tempt him, which she doubted. This marriage was conditional on their not having sex—why on earth would he break that clause on their first night together, thus making the ceremony they'd gone through a complete waste of time? If he'd wanted a sex-filled marriage then he would have chosen his American mistress, or somebody else he fancied like mad.

Her cheeks were flaming as she ran her wrists under the cold tap and tried to shut down her decadent thoughts. Drawing in a deep breath, she steeled herself for the onslaught to her senses as she returned to the bedroom. But she needn't have bothered because Zayed was no longer standing where she'd left him, bathed in moonlight. He was in bed, his hard body outlined perfectly beneath the thin white sheet, his dark head contrasted against the snowy pillow. As he slept, his powerful chest rose and fell with each even breath and she found herself envying his ability to blot everything out when she felt so churned up inside.

And then she remembered something else. Something which all the excitement and turbulence of the day had driven clean out of her head. Once again she was reminded of the look on his face as she'd entered the throne room. Not the initial disbelief, nor the brief flicker of lust—but something else. A dark and haunted look, steeped in pain and the faintest hint of vulnerability. She wondered if she should ask him about it, then wondered if she had the right. Not really. Zayed wasn't a puzzle she was supposed to gradually unpick. He was nothing to her, just as she was nothing to him.

But as Jane climbed silently into bed beside him she suspected a fretful night lay ahead of her, just as he had predicted.

CHAPTER SIX

SHE WAS WOKEN by a cry—a strange, guttural cry which sounded as if someone's soul were being ripped from their body. Jane sat bolt upright in bed and stared down at the man she'd married the day before, his rigid body washed with the silver moonlight which filtered in through the unshuttered tower windows. But this time she barely noticed his unclothed state—it was the terror etched deep on his hawkish features which captured her attention. He seemed not quite awake—but not asleep either—and as he cried out again the words were so broken that she couldn't work out their meaning. Jane swallowed, for although she'd seen Zayed Al Zawba in many different guises, she'd never imagined seeing him looking so vulnerable—or *scared.*

And she was scared, too. Scared of what to do. Scared to reach out to touch him when she'd never been in bed with a naked man before, let alone touched one. She recognised that he was caught up in his own private nightmare, which had contorted his face to an almost unrecognisable mask of pain, and suddenly compassion overrode all thoughts of self-preservation because she sensed he needed comfort and reassurance. He needed the warmth of human hands on his skin, helping release him from his bad dream.

Moving closer, her arms went round his tense body and she hugged him close, barely noticing the honed and silken flesh—so intent was she on helping soothe him. Gently she pulled his dark head to her shoulder, feeling the hot rush of his breath against her neck as he expelled a ragged sigh. Her fingers spread over his back, bringing him closer, willing him to relax.

'It's okay, Zayed,' she murmured gently, her fingers stroking their way through the tousled silk of his hair. 'It's going to be okay.'

Was it her words which broke the spell? Because just as rapidly as the tension had imprisoned him in that state of terror, it left him. She could feel it leaching from his body like air escaping from a balloon and her heart began to pound with relief. She wanted to carry on holding him and stroking his hair but she didn't dare. Because what if he woke up to find her clutching him and accused her of trying to seduce him, when they were supposed to be keeping their distance from each other?

So she rolled over and lay there in the moonlight, her heart still pounding as she waited to hear whether he'd say anything. But he didn't. She wondered if he was aware that she was holding her breath, or whether he'd even care if he knew what she'd just witnessed. She was still wondering what had caused the nightmare when eventually sleep claimed her and next time she opened her eyes it was to see Zayed sitting on the narrow window seat, his black gaze fixed intently on her as if he'd been studying her while she'd been asleep.

Had he?

He was fully dressed—his night-time nakedness now just a rapidly fading memory. This morning only his raven head was bare, his jaw darkened with the dark flush of stubble, and he was wearing riding clothes—close-fitting jodhpurs and a billowing white shirt. That would probably explain the sweat which beaded his forehead and the two flushed lines of colour painted along his high cheekbones. It was the first time she'd ever seen him dressed in anything other than his traditional robes and it was a distracting image. Macho and modern—he looked very slightly intimidating and one hundred per cent sexy. Even she, untouched and unwanted Jane Smith, could see that.

But she wasn't Jane Smith any more, was she? She was Jane Al Zawba, Sheikha of Kafalah and wife of its powerful ruler. And Zayed was her husband—the man who had cried out in the night and then lain briefly in her arms while she had comforted him. Would he mention what had happened? Could he even *remember* what had happened?

'So, my bride. Did you sleep well?' he questioned.

She met his gaze. They'd been honest with one another from the start and yet somehow she instinctively held back all the questions she wanted to ask. Because nobody ever liked revisiting nightmares, did they? It wasn't really any of her business because she wasn't a *real* wife. And it would hardly be the most glowing start to their already unconventional honeymoon if she started quizzing him about his night terrors. If he wanted her to know the reason behind them he would surely tell her. 'So-so,' she answered. 'How about you?'

His eyes gave nothing away. 'Fine,' he answered tightly, before rising to his feet and moving across the tower bedroom with panther-like grace towards a silver coffee pot which stood on a tray next to a pile of pastries.

She swallowed, aware that the fine white shirt was outlining the rocky silhouette of his torso. 'You've been riding,' she observed unsteadily.

Zayed nodded, aware of the sexual tension which had filtered into the atmosphere and aware of something else, too. Something which was stubbornly staying just out of reach at the edges of his mind. His night had been disturbed and the nightmare had come again in the same dark and fitful way it always did, leaving him empty and sad the next morning. He swallowed, his mouth growing dry, amazed that he hadn't woken Jane. Forcing his mind away from the darkness of the past, he saw that she was looking at him with widened eyes and realised she'd been asking him about horses.

'I have indeed been riding,' he said. 'I thought it probably best if I absented myself, in the circumstances. So I galloped over the sands and went out to watch the sun as it rose higher over the desert and began to paint the landscape with deep and uncompromising shadows.'

'It sounds beautiful.' He heard the wistfulness in her voice and briefly turned to look at her before pouring them each a cup of coffee.

'You don't ride?'

She shook her head. 'I grew up in a suburban house in west London. It wasn't exactly an area known for its love of the equine world.'

'Here,' he said, handing her a cup.

She took it and for a moment an unaccustomed mischief danced in her eyes. 'Do you always serve breakfast in bed?'

'Don't get used to it. This is a one-off. Yesterday was a long day so I arranged to have breakfast brought up here, but you slept through it. In fact, you weren't even roused by the knock of the maidservant.' He gave the ghost of a smile. 'No doubt that will fuel rumours that the bride is properly sated. So why don't you drink some coffee? It's strong enough to wake you and afterwards, we will eat.' He yawned. 'Even though my appetite is not *quite* as keen as it should be for a man on the first day of his honeymoon.'

'I think you've made your point, Zayed,' she said, sipping cautiously at the thick, sweet brew and finding it utterly delicious. 'There's no need to labour it.'

He thought how clever she was and how fearless in the way she spoke to him. 'Ah, Jane,' he said reflectively. 'Sometimes you have the barbed tongue of the desert serpent.'

Her voice was caustic. 'Thanks very much for the compliment.'

'Actually, it *is* a compliment. Didn't I once say that verbal sparring could be very *stimulating*?'

'Stimulation was not my intention.'

'No,' he said drily. 'I can tell. Which brings me neatly to my next point. Something I think we need to establish early on, to which I have only alluded before.'

'You can skip the build-up and just say whatever it is you want to say.'

'Very well.' His gaze was steady. 'Are you a virgin?'

Jane nearly spat out her coffee but composed herself in time. Her hand was trembling as she put the cup down on the table beside the bed and sat up. 'What right do you have to ask me a question like that?'

'Because you just told me to! And because I'm your husband.'

'Not my real husband! You're one half of a sexless marriage.' She glared at him. 'Why are you so interested?'

'Many reasons. Natural curiosity, for one. Perhaps because I've never spent the night with a virgin before. I've certainly never had sex with one.' He narrowed his eyes as if running through his memory. 'Or if I have, I wasn't aware of it.'

She screwed up her face. 'You're disgusting.'

'So you keep telling me,' he said softly. 'I've been called many things in my lifetime, Jane—but never that.'

'Probably because people are always treading carefully and kowtowing towards you because you happen to be a desert king.'

'It's possible,' he conceded, his gaze travelling over her, but there was open interest in his eyes rather than any element of flirtation. 'You think it's disgusting to talk about sex? For me to ask you something which I'd already suspected? That you are an innocent, which is rare enough in this day and age—but almost unheard of in a western woman of almost twenty-eight years. I admit I find it difficult to believe but my intention was not to make you feel like some kind of freak.'

She shook her head. 'That's not what's making me angry.'

'Then what is?' he challenged.

'You! The way you talk! The arrogant statements you keep coming out with. Telling me that you've never...*had* a virgin before! As if women were some kind of sport. What kind of a boast is that, Zayed?'

'It was a statement of fact,' he corrected. 'It was not intended as a boast. But talking about sex clearly bothers you.'

His voice had grown thoughtful and Jane looked down to see where his gaze was directed, horrified to notice that the sheet had slipped down to her waist, revealing breasts covered only in the delicate white silk of her nightgown. Breasts which seemed to have grown in size as well as in sensitivity. She could feel the aching hardness of their tips as she grabbed at the sheet to cover herself, trying to ignore the sound of his mocking laughter. Suddenly she felt hot and flustered and pleased that he hadn't woken up to discover her trying to comfort him.

'Are you trying to embarrass me, Zayed?' she demanded.

'No, Jane, I'm not. I was trying to establish a fact and to decide where we go from here. But I discover that I now find myself in a somewhat invidious position.'

She gazed at him suspiciously. 'Which is?'

He shrugged, and as he moved the billowing white silk shirt whispered against his skin. 'This is a marriage of convenience and you were chosen specifically because I did not find you attractive.'

'But suddenly you do?' she questioned sarcastically, hoping that would detract from her crushing insecurity.

'Actually, yes. Inexplicably and inconveniently, suddenly I do,' he agreed, and then he sighed. 'Perhaps it was the sight of you with Kafalahian emeralds in your hair, wearing that bridal gown which seemed to cling to every pore of your body.'

'How very superficial.'

'But men *are* superficial, Jane,' he argued. 'We are simple creatures, programmed to respond to very obvious stimuli. The tremble of a mouth stained with berries...the flutter of lashes around eyes which have been darkened with kohl. A body which you had never seen before—suddenly outlined as if by the loving detail of an artist's brush and revealing something underneath which is quite exquisite. Quite spectacular, if you must know. You looked beautiful on your wedding day and that is the image which has replaced the one I had of you before—of the woman in the shapeless clothes with her hair in a bun.' He shrugged in an apologetic gesture but the dark glint in his eyes didn't look remotely apologetic. 'And now I find that I cannot look at you without a hard and painful throbbing in my groin. It is a very...*uncomfortable* feeling.'

She would have chastised him with the most withering words in her vocabulary, if her cheeks hadn't been so red and if she hadn't suspected that it would fall on deaf ears. Because he wasn't seeking her praise or her approval, was he? He didn't *care* if she disapproved of the way he spoke to her. He was simply telling her what was on his mind. And yes, he was doing it in a manner which was brutally blunt— he certainly hadn't lifted his words from the pages of a diplomatic handbook! He made his physical reaction to her sound almost *anatomical*, which in a way, she supposed, it was. It shouldn't have been in the least bit flattering and yet...

Jane licked her lips. She couldn't deny the unexpected thrill of pleasure it gave her to know she was capable of arousing such a reaction in the Sheikh. To think that *she*, of all people, should make such a man experience desire. Was it that which gave her a brief taste of her own power? Which filled her with a sudden cool confidence as she tilted her chin to look at him? 'So deal with it.'

'How?'

'You're the expert. How do you *usually* deal with it?' she said, aware too late that she'd walked into some kind of trap, which she might have noticed if she hadn't been trying to distract herself from the squirmy feeling which was making her want to wriggle her bottom against the mattress.

His eyes glinted. 'My virgin bride is really asking me a question like that?'

'Stupid of me. You find a woman, I suppose. Only this time you can't because you've sworn off sex.'

'Often sex is a solution, yes.' He shrugged. 'But a woman is not always available—especially when I am in the desert.'

Another question she shouldn't have asked, but right then her heart was pounding so fast that she didn't really think it through.

'So then what?'

'Oh, come on. Work it out.' His black eyes gleamed as if registering the lack of comprehension on her face. 'I pleasure myself, of course.'

It took a moment for his words to sink in and when they did, Jane found herself blushing again. 'Oh,' she mumbled, all her earlier confidence crumbling away.

He studied her, as if he couldn't quite believe the implication of her reaction, and all at once his eyes were beseeching. 'Please tell me you don't deny yourself pleasure, Jane—even though you may have never known true intimacy with a man.'

Her colour deepened because unerringly he had hit on the truth—and how humiliating was *that*, because in this day and age wasn't it *doubly* shameful to be both a virgin and never to have experienced any kind of sexual pleasure? Especially when you lived in a society which was bombarded with sexual imagery. Her teeth dug into her bottom lip. Her reasons were complex and probably seemed stupidly old-fashioned, but sometimes circumstances helped create a situation which was not of its time.

How could she possibly explain that she'd always seen herself as clever Jane and plain Jane, just as everyone else had? That she'd helped care for her sick mother and stepped in when their father had gone to pieces afterwards? She'd cooked and cleaned and tried to dampen down her sister's wild and unpredictable nature—and in the midst of all that she'd done her best to study and work hard to gain the exams she'd needed. There hadn't been time for anything else—especially not the boys who'd looked straight through her because they'd been seduced by Cleo's abundant charms.

And when she'd gone to college, the only men she'd mixed with had been the tutors keen to capitalise on her eager intellect, or the occasional study partner she'd teamed up with in the university library. Her first fumbling experience on the college dance floor had been followed by another couple of dates with men who had left her completely cold. Perhaps she was simply guilty of preferring the fantasy desert lands she studied, which had made her unable to settle and uninterested in the whole dating scene.

She'd sublimated her own sexuality for so long that she didn't know if she was capable of feeling the things she knew most other women her age experienced. She'd never touched herself in the way to which Zayed was alluding because it had felt somehow...*wrong*. She was like someone who had never tasted sugar, who couldn't believe that sweetness existed. And now, with Zayed's black gaze piercing through her, she could feel herself start to bristle defensively.

'That's none of your business,' she said.

'I think it is my business. We're stuck with each other for six months and I think I need to know whether or not my wife has ever had an orgasm.'

Briefly Jane closed her eyes, telling herself to change the subject before the conversation got even more embarrassing. But reason wasn't strong enough to stem the suddenly powerful rush of her imagination. She thought about the erotic Kafalahian texts she'd been studying just before she'd come here, which she had read as matter-of-factly as if they'd contained reams of mathematical formulae. Within their heavy and beautifully illustrated pages had been acts which were completely alien to her. Things she'd never imagined would relate to her but which now began to invade her mind because somehow she could imagine *Zayed* doing them to her. Zayed's mouth upon her breast and Zayed's head between her thighs.

And she needed to pull herself together because such thoughts were insane. She needed to protect herself—in all ways. She mustn't get used to a level of intimacy which could never be sustained. Because within a few short months, she would be history and this man would be gone from her life for ever.

'I refer you to the terms of our agreement,' she said. 'And since we are in a short-lived marriage which forbids sex, I suggest we don't discuss it.'

'Why not?'

'Because it would seem to me, even with my vast inexperience, that to do so will make you increasingly frustrated. Wouldn't you agree? And now I think it might be best if you left me alone so that I can get dressed.'

His mouth twisting, Zayed rose to his feet. Her logic was infuriating but he couldn't fault it. And wasn't there a reluctant part of him which admired her cool intellect and powers of reasoning, even if his body was protesting at being kicked out of his honeymoon suite without so much as a glimpse of one cherry-topped nipple? 'Very well. I will leave you to get dressed,' he said tersely. 'Without feeling you have to hide away to prevent me from observing you in a state of undress. Heaven forbid I should see my wife naked!'

Frustration now pulsing through his veins like a fever, he wrenched open the door of the eastern tower and slammed his way out, knowing she had done nothing but speak the truth and not sure why he was so angry. Frustration, yes—but there was something else. Was it the fact that her will was strong? Maybe even as strong as his? That she hadn't given into temptation, even though she was obviously turned on by his presence? Probably. Or because he'd been left feeling as though she'd been the one calling the shots, when that was usually *his* role? Something else nagged at his mind too, but he was too full of exasperation to heed it.

Outside, the sun was much higher and he sucked in a breath of clear desert air, his gaze sweeping over the rose-gold of the palace walls, its cobalt domes contrasting with the paler blue of the sky. It was a sunny and beautiful day, but inside he felt as cold as ice. He found himself wondering if he would ever feel truly contented. Not happy, because he knew his limitations and happiness was something he'd never aspired to—for how could a heart know happiness when it had been ripped from his chest and crushed into a million pieces? But sometimes he wondered if he would ever experience the contentment which other men enjoyed.

His stocks and shares were riding high, his country was the world's fourth biggest exporter of oil and there had been no wars in the region for almost thirty years. His heart gave a savage twist of pain, because wouldn't his acquisition of Dahabi Makaan ensure that peace was likely to continue until the end of his reign, and beyond? He looked up at a distant bird of prey as it circled slowly in the thin air before poising to make its strike.

So where was this elusive thing called contentment—and why was its absence so glaringly apparent today, of all days? Was it because the strangely poignant words of the marriage ceremony had opened up the floodgates to feelings he'd been suppressing for as long as he could remember? Or because he found himself in uncharted territory—not simply because he was now a married man, but because he was dealing with a woman the like of whom he'd never known before.

He'd guessed Jane was a virgin but had failed to realise how sexually naïve she really was. Mightn't this bizarre situation have been easier if she *had* been more experienced? If she'd been one of those faintly cynical women he tended to favour. The ones who would do anything to accommodate his every need. His lips hardened. Perhaps not. It was easy to be bored by women like that. Sometimes he had made demands on them which had been thoughtless and cold. As if he was trying to test them. To push them to see just how far they would allow themselves to be pushed. And those women had always agreed to his requests, hadn't they? Had Jane been accurate when she'd claimed that people *kowtowed* to him because he was royal?

Yet Jane did not kowtow to him. She told him things straight. She answered him back, which nobody had ever done before. Part of him resented it but a much bigger part of him was tantalised by it— and surely that was dangerous. But he supposed he should be grateful that the last thing she did was *bore* him.

Slowly, he made his way back up the steep stone steps of the tower to discover his new wife dressed in some of the carefully selected robes which had been hurriedly assembled before their wedding. A selection of traditional Kafalahian royal garments had been provided as well as couture western clothes and it filled him with unexpected pleasure to note that she had chosen the former. A long, embroidered silk tunic the colour of new leaves skimmed her body— but, despite its relatively demure lines, he couldn't eradicate the vision of Jane in her wedding night lingerie, the slippery material clinging to every fleshy pore. He concentrated instead on the way she had pulled the hair tightly back from her face and wound it into the habitual bun.

'No, no, no,' he said, shaking his head. 'That will not do.'

He saw a faint look of disappointment cloud her eyes. 'I thought your people would prefer me to wear Kafalahian clothes while I'm here.'

'That isn't what I meant—and just for the record, the tunic suits you very well. It's your hair which is bothering me.'

She touched her fingertips to the tight bun. 'My hair?'

'Indeed. While you are with me, you will wear your hair down. If we want the world to believe in our union, it will be better if I don't appear to be married to someone who looks like some uptight librarian.'

'But I *am* a librarian, Zayed,' she said. 'Of sorts.'

'Not any more you're not,' he corrected. 'As of now you are my Sheikha and you will dress to please me.'

She opened her mouth to object but maybe she read the determination in his eyes, for slowly she unwound the bun and shook her hair free. He watched as it flowed down over the embroidered silk of her green tunic—a heavy fall of golden brown tumbling over her shoulders. A lump rose to his throat as his gaze flickered, mesmerised, to the pale oval of her face. He wondered what she would do if he kissed her. Well, he knew exactly what she would do. After an initial hesitation, her lips would open to allow the thrust of his tongue and then she would respond hungrily, if the expression in her eyes was anything to go by. His imagination began to fly. How long before her conscience forced her to stop him? he wondered. Long enough for him to explore beneath her tunic to discover if her panties were already wet? Long enough for him to peel them down and pleasure her with his finger, feathering it against her moist crack until she was screaming out in helpless pleasure?

He swallowed.

No. He must not allow himself to be distracted by lust. They had a deal and he would stick to it. And besides, wouldn't it give him an added power over her if he allowed her desire to simmer away without provocation? To let her discover the strength of his indomitable will in resisting her?

He flicked her a glance. 'We need to think about our honeymoon.'

'Yes.' She spoke carefully. 'It is a great honour to accompany you on a state visit to your embassy in Washington.'

His eyes narrowed as he heard the stilted quality of her words. Was she disappointed he hadn't taken her to one of the desert cities he suspected she craved to visit? Perhaps to the fabled and wondrous city of Qaiyama, with its ancient monuments and some of the country's oldest artwork? Well, that was too bad. He wasn't going to risk being alone in the romantic beauty of a Bedouin tent with her when he wasn't allowed to touch her.

Up until their wedding yesterday, Zayed wouldn't have cared *where* they had gone but he had witnessed some profound changes in his new wife over the last twenty-four hours. He had seen her body as no other man had ever seen it. He had spent the night with her even though they had not kissed, and that had been a first. He had discovered she was a stranger to pleasure but realised that her young and fertile body was instinctively crying out for a man like him to show her such pleasure, because the drive of the hormones was more powerful than the voice of reason.

This whole make-believe marriage was based on it not being consummated, but there was another reason why he could not contemplate being alone in the desert with her. Because Jane was the kind of woman who would never recover from a liaison with a man like him, if his will should weaken. He suspected she would become obsessed with him if he made love to her—and who could blame her? In many ways, he guessed he was her ideal man—he was the ruler of a country she adored. Like some fantasy figure from the pages of the manuscripts she spent her life deciphering, he had stepped into her life. He had transformed her into his Sheikha—and that was pretty stirring stuff for the Englishwoman. Just imagine if he allowed them certain intimacies... If she discovered what he was truly capable of in bed—or out of it. Why, she would spend the rest of her days heartsick and aching for him and he would not do that to her. He must not hurt her in that way.

Infused with a sudden sense of satisfaction at his own magnanimousness, he smiled. 'Yes, an honour indeed,' he said. 'Our embassy in Washington is eagerly anticipating our arrival and preparations are under way for a party to introduce you to the wider world. And we can enjoy the city, which has much to offer—have you ever been there before?'

She shook her head. 'No. I've never been to America.'

'It's a beautiful country—and there will be enough diversions for us to stop focussing on what we can't have, and concentrate instead on what we *can*. There are some rare texts you might be interested in looking at, while I can discuss the takeover of Dahabi Makaan with my advisors.' His mouth hardened as he looked at her. 'It might not be the most conventional honeymoon in the world but right now it's the only one on offer.'

CHAPTER SEVEN

WASHINGTON SEEMED SMALLER and more manageable than it looked in all the news broadcasts, though Jane suspected that she was seeing the city differently as the wife of one of the world's most powerful rulers. A red carpet awaited them when they touched down at Dulles International Airport and they were driven straight to the beautiful gilded building in Massachusetts Avenue, known as 'Embassy Row', which housed the Kafalahian Commission.

The welcome they were given was rapturous. All members of staff—both Kafalahian and local—had lined up to meet them and Jane wondered if she would ever get used to all this pomp and ceremony, before reminding herself that such fears were unnecessary. *You won't need to get used to it. It'll be over before you know it, so better not get too comfortable in your new role.*

At last they were taken to their suite. It was the first time they'd been alone all day and Jane kicked off her shoes and sank onto the huge bed, watching Zayed as he walked over to the desk. She wondered how the staff would react if they knew the truth about their marriage. If their welcome would have been quite so rapturous if they'd realised it was nothing but an empty farce—and that the sexy Sheikh of Kafalah would lie chastely by the side of his new bride that night and all the nights which followed.

But it was funny how even the strangest of situations became normal after a while. This was only their fourth day together as man and wife but already she was growing less self-conscious about being alone with Zayed. Adhering to an unspoken agreement not to test their resolve any more than was necessary, they went to bed at different times, and when she awoke in the morning he was always gone. At least he was able to lose himself in the hard exertion of a desert ride on one of his famous black stallions. Jane's diversions were more gentle in nature but they provided her with a welcome distraction.

In the few days before they'd left for Washington, she'd spent her days exploring the corridors of the rose-gold Kafalahian palace, putting in many hours in the library, before escaping into the beautiful gardens during the cooler, rose-scented evenings.

In many ways it should have been a dream come true—the culmination of all her academic endeavours—to be granted free access to a place she'd been learning about since she was eighteen. And yet it was strange how the human spirit could often defy expectation. How was it that the illuminated manuscripts, the exquisite statues and paintings were far less compelling than her thoughts about Zayed Al Zawba? She used to hate him, but somehow she couldn't seem to hate him any more. Perhaps it would have been easier if she did. But people were irrational and out of her initial animosity towards him had grown a complicated cocktail of feelings.

She found herself admiring his strong work ethic, his razor-sharp mind and obvious dedication to his people. He was encyclopaedic in his knowledge about his country and, for an academic like her, to be able to tap into such first-hand knowledge was truly exciting. She still felt she didn't really know him. He remained an enigma and that was clearly how he liked it. Yet beneath the implacability of the royal mask he wore was something dark. Something painful. She'd discovered that on their wedding night when that terrible dream had made his face become distorted and his body grow rigid with fear. And last night it had happened again.

Jane bit her lip. She'd woken to the sound of that broken cry as he'd uttered broken words she couldn't understand. His body had been bathed with sweat, his eyes wide open as he stared at the nameless thing which was haunting him—and once again she had cradled him for as long as it took for the demons to go on their way. Yet this morning his shuttered features had warned her to keep her distance, so that still she hadn't dared ask him the cause of the nightmare. She told herself it was no business of hers. She told herself she shouldn't care that he was hurting.

But she did.

The thought of the despair she'd seen in his eyes was so unexpectedly painful that she sucked in a sharp breath and Zayed turned to look at her, lifting his head from the stack of diplomatic papers he'd been flicking through.

He frowned. 'Something wrong?'

She shrugged. 'I'm a little nervous, I guess.'

'Of what?'

Of the pain I heard in your voice last night. Of the bleakness I saw in your eyes. She forced herself to be pragmatic. To be the bride she was expected to be. The cool-thinking academic who didn't think or behave like other women, not the clinging partner who demanded to know his every thought. 'Oh, come on, Zayed. You might be used to all this.' She made an expansive movement with her hand, which took in the billowing silk of the primrose-coloured drapes and the exquisite furniture inlaid with mother-of-pearl. 'But I'm not.'

He shrugged. 'I thought you were adapting pretty

well to the far more lavish setting of my palace in Kafalah.'

'That was different. I've studied Kafalah so much that I almost feel I've been there before. Here I feel as if we're on the world stage. And tonight I shall be dressed like a desert queen and brought in front of the city's finest and no doubt every female will be wondering how I could possibly have bagged myself one of the world's most eligible men.'

He put the pile of papers down. 'I thought we'd established—and which I thought I'd made very clear to you—that you've been looking beautiful since our wedding? Disturbingly so. I don't think anyone in their right mind will be wondering that. Did you see the coverage in this morning's papers, describing you as the jewel in Kafalah's crown?'

No, she hadn't seen it—even though there was a pile of neatly ironed international newspapers on the desk right next to all Zayed's official stuff, which she could have gone right ahead and looked at. But she didn't care about personal acclamation, prob-ably because none had ever come her way before now. And how could she possibly explain that it felt so empty? So *meaningless*. What was the point of looking beautiful for a man who wouldn't touch you? Who couldn't touch you. A man who kept his past hidden away, even though he knew so much about her. Wouldn't attending parties inevitably put them under the microscope? Wouldn't it enable people to see through them and discover the insubstantial core at the centre of their marriage—and thus risk making them a laughing stock?

'People are going to be watching us,' she said. 'Analysing our body language in the way that people do. They'll know our marriage is fake.'

'They won't *know*.'

'Then they'll guess.'

'So what is it you're asking?' he demanded. 'That I should shower you with kisses in public? Brush my fingers against your waist in an unseemly show of affection whenever there's a camera pointed in our direction? Build myself into an unbearable state of sexual frustration, knowing I can't act on it when we're alone again? Is that what you want, Jane?'

One word leapt out at her, dominating even the rather pleasing fact that he didn't *dare* touch her. 'Unseemly?'

His mouth twisted impatiently. 'I despise this idea that the image we present to the outside world is who we really are. It's what makes social media so dangerous. I won't play-act the part of lovestruck groom and risk ridicule when our marriage is quietly dissolved in a few months' time. I can only be the man I really am.'

She stared at him, frustration vying with admiration because so many of his traits appealed to her, even though she didn't want them to. He was so proud. So indomitable. So utterly sure of himself. *And yet didn't his nightmares contradict some of that swaggering assurance? As if at the heart of Zayed Al Zawba was a dark vulnerability so much at odds with the man he presented to the world.* Was it so wrong to want to understand the person behind the King she'd married? She'd told him stuff about herself but so far he hadn't reciprocated.

'You realise I know practically nothing about you,' she said.

He raised his eyebrows. 'On the contrary—you know more than most people. You know all about my ancestors and their history.'

'That's not what I meant and you know it. I'm serious, Zayed.'

'And so am I, Jane. Deadly serious. I don't talk about myself. I don't bare my soul—not to you, not to anyone.'

She knew that it was pointless to say *But I'm your wife* because she wasn't—not in any way that counted. So she tilted her chin and stared straight into the night-dark beauty of his eyes instead. 'Why not?'

He shrugged his powerful shoulders. 'Because trust is an issue and a lot of people in my position feel the same.' He hesitated. 'Being royal is different. You risk too much when you let people close. Because people will betray you, or sell-out.'

'You don't trust me?'

There was a pause. 'Actually, I *do* trust you. I don't know why, but I do.' His glance was impatient, as if he wanted the conversation to be over. 'But there is little point in telling you the things I suspect you want to know.'

'Why not?'

'Because telling you stuff would indicate that I wanted a deeper level of understanding between us, and I don't.'

For some reason that hurt far more than it should have done but Jane kept her expression implacable. 'Or perhaps it might help release some of the demons which are locked up inside you.'

His body tensed. 'I don't have any demons, Jane.'

'Don't you?' she questioned quietly. 'Have none of the previous women you've slept with ever asked why sometimes you have nightmares? Why your body tenses up and you shout out strange and muffled things in the middle of the night? Things I don't understand but which chill my blood every time I hear them.'

Zayed stilled as he stared into the open gaze of her amber eyes, trying to dampen down the flare of anger and indignation. He'd thought the nightmares had ended. Had prayed they had—and that the one he'd had on his wedding night had been an aberration. Logic told him they were nothing but a recurring pattern—dark dreams kick-started by key emotional events in his life, but which would soon pass. And they did. It was just that every time they came back they were worse than the time before. The place they took you to was more unendurable. The residual feeling they left was behind was even more bitter. Maybe because the older you got the more you realised how much you had lost. Realised, too, just what you had failed to do… 'No,' he said roughly. 'They don't ask me and if they dare try, then I shut them down.'

'And they let you, I suppose. They let you do whatever you want because they don't want to displease you.'

'Something like that.' He gave a bitter laugh. 'Whereas you don't seem to care about displeasing me, do you, Jane?'

'That isn't my aim. I just don't see the point in tiptoeing around you,' she said, touching her fingertips to the diamond studs which were fixed to her ears, as if checking they were still there, before fixing him with a steady look. 'We already have enough areas in our lives which are off-limits without adding any more. Don't we?'

A great silence rolled between them, as big as those great waves which used to swell up on Azraq al-Haadi beach during the family holidays he and his parents used to take before the only world he'd ever known had been destroyed one springtime, when the desert had been carpeted with wildflowers. Zayed met the question in Jane's steady gaze. Why wasn't he silencing her with a curt command that she know her place, and why was the temptation to tell her tugging at him, like a kite being tugged by the insistent wind? He swallowed, knowing that such a disclosure would break a taboo, for he had never discussed it with anyone. Not even with his father, though he suspected he must have guessed at some of the things he'd been too stricken to hear at the time.

'You get one question, Jane,' he gritted out. 'That's all. What do you want to know?'

There was a moment's pause. 'What causes the nightmares?' she said eventually.

He had underestimated her intelligence. How very short-sighted of him. She was clever enough to realise that this one deceptively simple question would open up a whole web of explanation. He thought about prevarication. About inventing something to pacify her. But even if he'd wanted to, he could not lie to her, and not just because theirs was a relationship which had been grounded in brutal honesty right from the start. Something told him that those clear amber eyes would see right through him if he did.

'It's a long story.'

'We have plenty of time, Zayed,' she said softly.

He took her point. They were alone in their suite—some might say trapped. There was no vast palace at his disposal to escape to. No nearby stallion quickly saddled up for the man who longed to pound away his emotions with a hard ride across the desert sands.

He moved restlessly, his robes whispering against his skin as he walked towards the windows overlooking the embassy gardens, where the manicured lawns were bathed in golden sunlight and in the distance he could hear one of the embassy dogs barking. She was right. There was plenty of time. Almost too much.

'You know that my mother died when I was seven?'

Her face serious, she nodded. 'She was involved in a riding accident, wasn't she?'

A strange laugh was torn from his throat. 'You could say that. Some of the facts you will know—others you won't. Because much of what really happened is not documented in the record books.'

'Why not?' She sounded aghast and he could tell that for someone like her—who'd spent a whole life painfully constructing historical accuracy—to hide the truth away would be the worst kind of crime. But this was nothing to do with her work. This was strictly personal.

He sighed and shot her a warning look. 'If I tell you, you're not going anywhere with this information, Jane. I'm telling you as my wife and not as an historian—do you understand?'

'Yes,' she said again. 'I understand.'

He pulled in a deep breath. 'You know that my mother was promised to the King of Mazbalah?'

She nodded and he could see the interest sparking from her eyes. 'Yes. I knew that.'

'They'd been betrothed since they were children in what was seen as a political unification of two powerful dynasties. Both families wanted it—some might say pushed for it. It was an eagerly anticipated union and the celebrations were planned to set the desert world alight, but just before the wedding she met my father at an official function and they...' The words were drawn reluctantly from his lips, because he hated saying them. Hated acknowledging their power. For they represented the thing which most people craved for—the thing which had the ability to wreak so much havoc in its wake. His mouth twisted. 'They fell in *love*. Even though my mother's father despised the Kafalahian line and was eager for her to marry into the Al Haadi family, that did not deter them. They acted impetuously—some might say rashly. On the very morning of her intended wedding, my parents eloped.'

'This much I knew,' said Jane quietly. 'But I thought her jilted fiancé gave the pair his blessing?'

'Initially, he did. It was described by the courtiers as a magnanimous gesture in the light of the seemingly inevitable, but ultimately it was to save face in what must have been a monumental humiliation.'

His voice tailed off as dark pain speared through him and he could see the concern on her pale features. He wanted to snarl at her that he wasn't going to answer any more of her damned questions but at the same time he wanted to kiss her—as if a punishing and passionate kiss would have the power to wash away these bitter memories. *He'd never even kissed her*, he found himself thinking. What an idiot he was. Why the hell hadn't he done *that* instead of stepping back into a past he'd tried to leave behind a long time ago? Distracted her with ripples of pleasure instead of capturing her clever mind with facts. But he was in too deep to stop now. It was as if he'd removed the cork from a bottle which had been fermenting for decades—to discover that the wine inside was unbearably acrid as it bubbled over to escape.

'Despite being ostracised by her parents, my mother was soon accepted by the Kafalahian people who grew to love her, and for seven years we lived as a normal family,' he continued. 'Even if it was a royal one. My parents' only sadness was that the large brood of children they longed for never happened and I remained an only child.'

'So were you *lonely*?' she questioned.

He jerked his head back, unprepared for a question nobody had ever asked him before. Yes, he had been lonely, even though there had been countless distractions for the much-loved son of the royal couple—with horses and toys and the offspring of the local high born to play with whenever he wished. But he had felt excluded from the powerful circle of his parents' passion. Their love for each other had burned so fiercely that sometimes it had made you want to screw your eyes up against that bright light. His mouth hardened. And hadn't the strength of that passion made him wary of such love, hating its all-consuming power and the way it razed away everything in its path?

'Sometimes,' he said, in as honest an admission as he'd ever made.

'Go on,' she said quietly.

He shook his head as if to clear it. 'When I was seven, my father had to go away to Maraban on business—so my mother took me to one of our houses high in the mountains, in the western reaches of Kafalah. I remember it as being a perfect holiday, because it was a spectacular springtime, when for once the wildflowers were all in bloom. In the mornings she used to take me fishing in one of the mountain streams and we would picnic there afterwards. It was such a quiet and peaceful place that we required less than the usual quota of bodyguards. Or so we thought.' His mouth hardened as his words tailed away and he found himself lost in the painful landscape of what had happened, wondering if they'd been naïve to have considered themselves so safe.

'Zayed?' she prompted cautiously.

He forced himself to continue because he had given his word that he would answer her question, but it was more than that. Suddenly he found himself wanting to expose the poison and the guilt to her and, yes, the shame. The bitter shame which would never leave him. Would Jane despise him for what he had done as much as he despised himself?

'The jilted king came for my mother. His anger brewing and brewing, he had been biding his time for the perfect moment to take her back and now he had found it. She saw him from a distance riding up the mountain towards us and I saw fear in her face. Fear like I'd never seen before. She called for the bodyguards, but none came. Her fingers dug into my arms as she whispered into my ear and told me I must hide away and not make a sound. That I must be as quiet as if my life depended on it. I will never forget the way her voice sounded, or the urgency with which she spoke. And because I loved my mother and because I was too young to know any better, I did exactly as she said. I folded myself into the dark crevice of a cave and waited.'

He clenched his hands into fists, staring down at their white-knuckled definition as if they belonged to someone else. 'And they came for her,' he continued hoarsely. 'I heard the vicious curses they made as they took her away but she made no sound. She went willingly to her fate. And it was long after I heard the last of the horses' hooves thundering back down the mountain path that I ran out to search for the guards.'

His voice tailed off as he felt the powerful punch of pain to his chest.

'Zayed?' she said, again.

'I found them mutilated,' he said, his voice shaking with helpless rage. 'Still alive but with their legs broken so they couldn't mount a chase. There were no mobile phones then, of course. We had no instant means of communication. We were essentially helpless on the mountainside.'

'So what did you do?'

'Darkness was falling as I saddled up one of the horses and rode to the nearest village. I got lost several times along the way and it was almost morning by the time I got there, when all hell broke out. My father returned from Maraban and organised groups of men to search and find my mother.'

Jane closed her eyes. She knew the end to this story for it was well documented. Zayed's mother had been found lying dead after a rock had fallen on her during the long ride back to Mazbalah. A rock which had hit her skull and crushed it, like a melon. But up until this moment, she'd never known the reasons why. The abduction had never made it into the historical documents and the vagueness of the facts had enabled the establishment to make it sound like a terrible accident. Slightly confused, she looked across the sumptuous suite at Zayed, silhouetted so still against the window, his shadowed face ravaged with pain.

'And your father?' she whispered.

He let out a long and ragged sigh. 'He caught up with the King and challenged him to a duel and inflicted a fatal blow to his heart,' he said grimly. 'But in so doing—was himself mortally injured. They brought him back to the palace, where I spent those last hours by his bedside.'

'Oh, Zayed.' She clamped her fingertips over her lips as she pictured the scene. A little boy of seven, still grieving for his mother, while his father lay dying in front of him in the vastness of that gilded Kafalahian palace. What terrible loss and pain he had known at such an early age—why, it made her own fractured childhood seem like nothing. Instinctively she got up from the bed and walked across the room towards him because the distance between them seemed too great to say what she wanted to say. And when at last she was standing in front of him and could see the indescribable sadness in his black eyes, she whispered out the hopelessly inadequate words. 'I'm so sorry.'

He inclined his head in a stately gesture as he acknowledged them.

'Do you want to tell me what happened next?'

There was a pause before he nodded, his accented voice shattering the silence. 'My father told me that what was done was done, and that was to be an end to it. He made me promise never to seek any more vengeance, nor to risk spilling my own blood for a cause that was now lost, because it would break my mother's heart if I were to do so—and nothing could ever bring her back. One of the reasons we deliberately kept the circumstances so vague afterwards was to deter rival factions in either country from seeking revenge.'

'That's why you were brought up by courtiers as the youngest regent monarch the region had ever known,' she said slowly.

'Yes.' There was a pause. 'And that was what caused the final severing of my relationship with my grandfather. His daughter had been his heart's joy. He blamed the Al Zawba family for interfering with her destiny and causing her death, and maybe he was right. If she hadn't listened to her heart, she might be alive now. If she hadn't married my father she would probably have lived to a ripe old age—'

'Zayed, you can't *know* that.'

'Can't I?' His voice had become fierce. 'Perhaps she would also have lived if I hadn't listened to her instructions to hide myself away. If I had gone after them, or challenged the King—'

'What? A seven-year-old boy, challenging a king?'

'And why not?' he argued fiercely. 'Mightn't it have struck at his conscience to realise just what he was doing by removing a mother from her son? But instead I just hid away, like a coward. I hid longer than I needed to hide. Too frozen with fear to dare to emerge.'

'You did what you did because your mother asked it of you,' she argued. 'You achieved what any mother would have wanted for her child...you kept yourself *alive*.'

He gave a bitter laugh. 'Yes. I lived so that I might remember what I had done.'

She shook her head. 'No, Zayed. Deep down you must realise that isn't true. Just as you must realise that your grandfather must have been seeking to make amends for his anger by leaving you Dahabi Makaan in his will—and you were big enough to accept that offer and to offer him your hand on his deathbed. Can't you just concentrate on that—on the good things which eventually emerged from such a terrible situation? Because that's all we can do in life, to make the best out of the bad things.'

Zayed nodded. She was standing in front of him and in that moment he thought she'd never looked more beautiful. Maybe it was because her amber eyes were shining with fervour—as if her peace-making passion had the ability to cleanse his troubled soul. Did it? Had the telling of his story lessened some of its power over him? He wondered if the old saying was true—that a problem shared was a problem halved. And it wasn't really a problem any more, was it? He had done what his mother had asked. Done what his father had asked, too. By the time he'd reached manhood there had been no vengeance left in Zayed's blood—and no desire for subsequent wars with innocent lives lost. He had honoured all his promises—and if that had left him with an empty space where his heart should have been, was it really so surprising?

'I repeat my demand that this goes no further,' he said grimly. 'I don't want you writing up some learned essay on the subject after our divorce.'

'I wouldn't dream of doing that.' She flinched. 'You told me that you trusted me.'

'Yes.' But at that moment he felt more than trust. He felt desire. He could feel it flooding his veins. Like honey, it thickened his blood and pooled to harden at his groin as he stared into the face of his bride. The autumnal sunshine made her hair resemble gleaming gold and he wanted to brush his lips over its silken spill. And more. Couldn't he pull her into his arms? Bend his head and lose himself in the softness of her lips? Kiss her hard until she was writhing in his arms, wanting more? His mouth dried. Yet the crazy thing was that he didn't really *do* kissing. It was almost too intimate an act of foreplay, which gave women unrealistic expectations. Kissing made them buy into the fairy tale of love, which he was incapable of delivering. He preferred the baring of breasts or that first indefinable taste, when you put your head between a woman's thighs and licked her until she came in your mouth.

Yet he could sense that Jane was hungry for him, too. He could feel the answering desire which was radiating from her curvy body. Temptation washed over him and his groin grew even harder as he thought about just giving in. For a split second he tensed, seeing the hopeful darkening of her amber eyes as if she anticipated what he was about to do. And never in his life had he wanted a woman more than he did right then.

Until he remembered their deal.

No consummation meant a simple dissolution of their marriage and that was the way he wanted it.

The only way it could possibly be.

'Why don't you freshen up after your journey?' he suggested and watched her body jerk, like someone who'd been stung. 'I have papers which need my attention before tonight's reception.' He gave her a cool smile before walking back over to the desk. 'And you'll need to pretty yourself up before the party, won't you?'

CHAPTER EIGHT

JANE FELT HURT, even though she told herself she had
no right to be. She tried to rationalise her thoughts in
a way which usually came as easily to her as breathing but for once it was proving difficult. Okay, so
Zayed had pushed her away straight after he'd taken
her into his confidence and told her the full and
shocking facts about his mother's death. He'd been
cold towards her at a time when they could have been
close, when she could have offered him comfort. *But
why was she hankering after closeness* when he'd
explicitly said he didn't want it? He'd told her about
his past because she'd asked him about the nightmares, that was all.

And no, he hadn't kissed her, even though the
expression in his black eyes had suggested he
might. Why *would* he kiss her, when no sex was
what explicitly defined their marriage? She should
just be glad he'd trusted her enough to tell her what
had really happened to his mother and father. Her

heart should be full of empathy for his terrible experience.

And it was. It was brimming over with sorrow for what he'd suffered. She wanted to put her arms around him and hug him tightly as she'd done on their wedding night, but she didn't dare. Because she was aware that sexual desire was growing with each second she spent in his company.

She could feel it in the heaviness of her breasts as she soaped them in the shower while getting ready for the official reception and in the restless ache between her thighs. At one point, impulse made her run her middle finger experimentally between her legs and she shivered before snatching it away again—scared of the intense physical sensations it provoked. Why now? she wondered desperately. Why should her body have tantalisingly come to life when she was trapped with a man who couldn't touch her?

Wrapping herself in a snowy bathrobe, she padded into the dressing room to study the selection of clothes which had been flown out from Kafalah. Row upon row of them were lined up—exquisitely embroidered silk tunics, all with matching trousers. There were western clothes, too. Couture dresses designed to fit like a glove. Slim skirts and gossamer-fine blouses. Shoes with spiky heels and silk stockings to wear with them, although so far she hadn't tried either. Since they'd married she'd dressed as a Kafalahian woman but tonight she didn't feel like one. She felt like an outsider. A cuckoo in the nest. A woman with no real place in this strange new royal world she found herself in.

Was it that which made her ignore the Kafalahian tunics and pull on a shimmering floor-length dress in black, which was the ultimate in glamour and sophistication? She stepped back from the mirror, slightly alarmed to see that the designer gown was doing things to her body she hadn't thought possible. The fabric clung to every pore, lifting and separating her breasts yet at the same time magically making her look as if she'd lost ten pounds. Her hair she left loose, clipping back the front strands with two of the glittering diamond clips she assumed Zayed would like to see her wearing.

She didn't hear him enter the dressing room and for once she barely registered the towel covering his groin and buttocks, because she'd become used to that, too. Didn't matter how big the towel was, it never seemed big enough for Zayed.

Tonight it was the look in his eyes which commanded her attention as it travelled in disbelief down her body before drawing her gaze to his, like a black flame sucking her in, the ebony fire flickering over her and growing in intensity. She waited for him to say something but he didn't and as the silence grew insecurity plagued her—just as it had plagued her all her life. 'You don't like it?' she said.

'Don't *like* it?' He gave an odd kind of laugh. 'What on earth gives you that idea?'

She shrugged her shoulders awkwardly. 'Because you didn't say anything—and I can't quite work out the expression on your face.'

'That's good. I don't particularly want you to *work out* the expression on my face,' he said obscurely. 'But if you really want to know what I'm thinking, it's that you're going to make every man in the room tonight want to possess you.'

Her hand flew to cover the shadowed line of her cleavage. 'That wasn't what I intended,' she whispered hoarsely. 'You think it's too much?'

'Not at all. The dress is perfectly decent, just that on you it looks…' He shook his head. 'I can't quite put my finger on it. Maybe it's because it's a very sexy dress and you're a total stranger to sex, and I'm the only one who knows that. Perhaps it's the contrast of the pure and the provocative which makes it so captivating.' He cleared his throat. 'And since I'm about to get dressed myself, maybe you'd like to turn away—just like you always do—that is, unless you want to catch a glimpse of my naked body which is currently in a very uncomfortable state of arousal.'

And wasn't it crazy that for once she was tempted to call his bluff. To stand there and say insouciantly,

okay, go ahead while she dared to look at all that
honed and tawny skin. Because wasn't her natural
curiosity growing in tandem with her increasing
frustration? Hadn't she started wondering what it
would be like to have an orgasm—her face perhaps
wearing that dreamy look of bliss afterwards which
she'd seen on the faces of the women in those erotic
Kafalahian drawings?

A lump rose in her throat. It was as if marriage
to Zayed had made her look at her life and see all
the things which were missing. She'd started to realise that if she wasn't careful she could lock herself
away until it was too late to enjoy some of the many
pleasures available to her. All her youth and zest for
living could just drain away, like the sand slowly
trickling through an egg-timer. She could bury her
head in her textbooks to her heart's content but one
day she might look up to discover wrinkles on her
face and a wizened body no man would ever want.

With a sigh, she went over to the window and
watched a gardener raking up a few fallen leaves to
add to a growing pile and when she turned round
again, Zayed was dressed.

'You're wearing a suit,' she said, surprised.

'Given your own choice of wardrobe, I thought it
might make us look less mismatched,' he said drily.

'Even if we are?'

He raised his eyebrows before unclipping the lock

of a slim, leather box she'd only just noticed he was holding. 'I think we can do our best to put on a unified front on our first social engagement as a married couple. And here is something which will indicate your significance in my life, Jane.'

Before she could challenge him on *that*, he had pulled out a necklace from its bed of indigo velvet, lifting it up in a dazzle so bright that it actually made Jane blink as she stared at it in disbelief. Hanging from a glittering jet choker was a pear-shaped diamond as big as a giant teardrop and Jane thought she'd never seen anything quite so beautiful as she realised what she was looking at.

'The Kafalahian Star!' she gasped.

He nodded. 'You know of it?'

Her throat felt so tight she could barely speak. 'Of course I do. But I've only ever seen pictures of it. I didn't even realise you'd brought it with you. I mean…it's been in your family for centuries, hasn't it?' She touched her fingers to her neck. 'Gosh. I don't know if I can wear it, Zayed.'

'Why not?' He moved behind her to wind the choker around her neck and once again she was acutely conscious of the brush of his fingers. 'Every Kafalahian Queen wears the Star for her first formal outing.'

'It's exquisite,' she said slowly. But as her finger traced over the teardrop diamond she found herself thinking how shallow women could be. Even her, with all her supposedly lofty ideals, could be dazzled by the shiny sparkle of a pretty jewel!

Their eyes met in the mirror and she identified the smoky darkening of his. When he looked at her that way it made her stomach turn to mush. It made her want to lean back against him and feel the warmth which radiated from his powerful body, but already he was moving away and opening the door with a faintly imperious gesture.

'Come on. Let's go.'

And then they were descending the swooping curve of the grand staircase to the smattering of applause from the waiting guests below. Musicians struck up the opening chords of the Kafalahian national anthem as they walked into the vast ballroom and they both stood very still until the haunting melody had finished.

Jane was introduced to countless people that night, but all she could think about was the dark king by her side. A man who, for all his earlier confidences, now seemed as cool and distant as a stranger. And wasn't the crazy thing that those confidences had whetted her appetite and made her want more of that kind of closeness, even though she knew she wasn't going to get it?

She tried to put it out of her mind as she met with the glittering Washington crowd she guessed must frequent these kinds of parties. Her mouth was aching from smiling and she was hopeful she'd produced a convincing performance as the monarch's consort but soon she began to long to escape from the chatter and the crowd. On her way back from the restroom, she took the opportunity to grab a moment's respite by relaxing behind the privacy of a marble pillar when she was startled by the sound of a vaguely familiar English voice behind her.

'Jane?'

It was strange, hearing someone use her first name when she was quickly getting used to people referring to her by one of her royal titles. She turned round to see a tall, geeky-looking man in dark-rimmed glasses standing there—a slightly amused smile on his lips.

She screwed up her eyes as a long-ago memory stirred. 'Hello,' she said, half questioningly.

'You don't remember me?'

And suddenly she did. It was David Travers, who'd studied at the School of Oriental and Asian Studies with her and shared her passion for the east. He'd been a 'geek' just like her, though Jane had reflected at the time that male geeks were much more popular than their female equivalent. Similarly ambitious, the two of them had spent long hours together, burning the midnight oil in the library, before they'd lost contact after leaving university.

'Of course I remember you,' she said, her smile

widening. 'It's just a bit weird seeing you here—a blast from my past, when everything is mainly about my husband.'

'Not nearly as weird as it is for me seeing the super academic Jane Smith looking like, well…like a queen!'

She smiled. 'How lovely to see you again, David. What are you doing these days?'

He returned her smile as he walked over to join her. 'I'm here in an official capacity. I work in Washington. I joined the Foreign Office after college and thought I'd done rather well for myself, but I must say that you've exceeded all expectations. A sheikha, no less.' His eyes narrowed. 'How are you, Jane?'

Only someone who had known you when you had nothing could have asked such a candid question and for a moment Jane couldn't think quite how to answer. Could he read the uncertainty in her eyes? Could she bluster enough to convince him she was happy?

'I'm fine,' she said breathlessly, even though she didn't feel it. Because how could she tell him the way she *really* felt—uncertain about her future and her growing feelings for the man she'd married? Feelings which were going to end up hurting her if she allowed them to. She forced a smile—the same cool, queen-like smile she'd been giving all evening. 'Absolutely fine.'

'Well, you look amazing—I hardly recognised

you at first,' David said quietly. 'Though if you'll forgive me for saying so—a little pale.' He hesitated. 'Look, would you like to go and stand outside on the balcony? I think it's still warm enough—and the view is pretty amazing from there.'

From his vantage point on the opposite side of the ballroom, Zayed watched Jane slip outside with a man he didn't know and was startled by the dark and inexplicable rush of jealousy which flooded through him. Inexplicable because he didn't *do* jealousy. Just as he didn't do baring his soul and talking about stuff from the past which was better left deep inside. But he had done all that, hadn't he? Had allowed his wife to glimpse the man beneath the royal façade and was now bitterly regretting letting his tongue run away with him.

He could see her on the balcony, the wind making her hair shimmer as the stranger in glasses moved a little closer. Zayed turned his head and gave the merest elevation of his eyebrows—a gesture which was correctly interpreted by one of his staff, who came scurrying over, to inform him that the sophisticated-looking man in glasses was a diplomat at the British Embassy.

His aide spoke in rapid Kafalahian. 'You wish me to remove him from the side of the Queen, Your Highness?'

'No,' said Zayed tersely. 'I have no wish to cause any kind of scene. As it happens, I am growing a little weary. The Sheikha and I will retire before the night is much older.'

But a lifetime of protocol was hardwired into Zayed's system and he forced himself to endure the rituals which were expected of him. Rituals so familiar he felt he could have performed them in his sleep. He'd been to hundreds of parties like this, though never with a new bride. Not that such a change in his marital status deterred the glamorous heiresses who made it clear they were more than eager to enjoy his body between the sheets. But Zayed had no appetite for brazen blondes with fake breasts and lustrous lips. His interest was not stirred by their predatory expressions or louche intentions. All he could focus on were the shadowy outlines of his virginal wife and the man with whom she stood talking on the balcony.

At last he could bear it no longer and he walked outside to see Jane's hair being lifted from her cheeks by the light breeze and the sparkle of the Kafalahian Star rivalling the glittering stars overhead. And suddenly all his self-belief that he was not a jealous man was vanquished by the burst of sheer possessiveness he experienced as he saw her curvy body, outlined in the black dress. He could feel the wild thunder of his blood. Was that guilt he read on her face as she turned and saw him? he wondered grimly. Why else did she bite her lip and stop speaking as soon as he appeared?

'Zayed!' she said at last, fixing a bright smile to her lips. 'I'd like to—'

'We're leaving, Jane.'

'But—'

'Now,' he said, with silken emphasis, aware of the faint look of surprise on the face of her companion, but suddenly he didn't care if he was breaking some damned *protocol*.

Zayed could hear her saying something to the man, but his blood was pounding so loudly in his temples that he couldn't make out what it was. He said nothing as they bade goodnight to the Ambassador, nor as they mounted the sweeping staircase in silence, the fading strains of music from the ballroom the only sound he could hear, other than the loud thunder of his heart. But as soon as he'd dismissed the discreet posse of bodyguards who had followed them and shut the door of their suite, he turned to her, unable to dampen his outrage.

'What do you think you were playing at?' he demanded hotly. 'Behaving in such an inappropriate way?'

But if he was expecting contrition, he was quickly disappointed because she rounded on him with nothing but anger spitting from her amber eyes.

'I could say the same for you!' she retorted. 'I

can't believe you acted that way. Stomping up to me and dragging me away like some sort of caveman. You were so *rude*!'

'Please don't presume to lecture me on courtesy,' he responded icily. 'And let me ask you instead why you sneaked off to be alone with a man who is unknown to me?'

'And whose fault is that? You didn't exactly hang around so I could introduce you, did you?'

'That isn't the point, Jane.'

'No? Then what *is* the point? Would you prefer to choose everyone I'm allowed to speak to for the duration of our so-called *marriage*?'

'Let's just keep to the salient facts,' he bit back. 'What were you saying, which required so much secrecy, which required you to sneak out onto the balcony in order to say it?'

She shook her head and stared at the carpet. 'That wasn't why we went outside.'

'I want to know.'

She lifted her chin and he could read the defiance on her face. 'David is an old friend from university and we have lots in common—mainly a love of ancient literature. We used to study together in the university library. He's a nice person. I simply hinted that some time in the future we might be friends again.'

'Friends?' he shot out. 'Or more than friends?'

'Who knows?' She shrugged but the anger was

still sparking from her eyes. 'Who knows what the future holds when I am no longer your Queen?'

'And did you tell him the truth about our marriage? Did you give him a timetable of our chaste nights and impending divorce so that he could start ticking off the days until you could leap into his bed?'

'Of course I didn't! We just had a normal conversation and it helped me come to a conclusion which has been bubbling away ever since I agreed to be your wife.' She sucked in a deep breath and pulled back her shoulders. 'I've realised I can't go on the way I have been doing, just existing in the shadows, like a ghost of a woman. I've realised that once this is all over, I want to get out there and start *living*. I want to be a real woman,' she finished slowly.

'Is that a euphemism for having sex?'

There was a pause and when she met his eyes her expression was fearless. 'Well, why not?' she challenged, her voice low and true. 'I doubt whether you'll be signing a pledge of chastity after we get divorced, will you, Zayed? I'm not planning to be a virgin *all* my life.'

He could hear the sound of heavy breathing and realised it was his own, just as he realised that the erection pressing against his trousers was harder than anything he'd ever felt before. He could feel the pounding of his heart and knew he shouldn't do what he was about to do but somehow he just couldn't stop himself. He reached out and caught her in his arms, seeing the instant darkening of her eyes and the frantic pulse which was beating at her temple as he pulled her against him. With his thumbs he smoothed back her hair, their roughened pads brushing against each diamond clip as he stared down into her face.

'What are you doing, Zayed?' she croaked, her tongue snaking out to moisten her lips as if to prepare them in readiness for him.

'What I should have done weeks ago,' he said, lowering his mouth to hers.

Jane felt her breath catch and her heart begin a giddy dance as Zayed began to kiss her. And after all the weeks of frustration, all she was aware of was an immense sensation of *joy* because if she was being brutally honest—hadn't she dreamed of this moment? Yes, she had. Night and day and at the most inappropriate moments, she'd wondered what it would be like to be in Zayed Al Zawba's arms like this. She'd always imagined that his kiss would be brutal. That it would be hard and possessive and masterful, just as he was. That it would crush her into sexual submission by showing her exactly who was boss and who had all the experience. But she had been wrong, because this was no such thing. It was a tantalising brush which was barely there. A slow, sensual invitation as his mouth grazed hers and

sent her senses spinning. 'Oh,' she breathed, disbelieving wonder distorting her voice as she clutched
his shoulders, like someone who was in danger of
sliding to the ground. *'Oh.'*

He drew back his head, his black eyes dazed
as they focussed on hers. 'Did you enjoy that, my
Queen?' he questioned unsteadily.

What was the point in lying? Why not face up
to the truth of her feelings? 'More than you'll ever
know,' she said softly.

She saw the flicker of fire in his eyes as he resumed the kiss in a more intimate re-enactment of
what had just taken place. This time his tongue flickered over her teeth, until they opened to grant him
access and he deepened the kiss. And now she was
on completely different territory. She was the pup-
pet and he the master—producing in her a reaction
which she didn't know she was capable of. She could
sense it in her spiralling response—in the way she
wriggled her hips restlessly against the hard cradle of
his, as if she were performing some ancient kind of
dance which she knew without having been taught.
Suddenly Zayed made a low, growling sound in the
back of his throat before picking her up and carrying her over to the bed. She could see the tension on
his hawkish features as he laid her down, just as she
could feel the urgent swelling of her breasts in response. Her body felt as if it had suddenly become too

big for the dress she was wearing—as if her breasts were going to burst right out of the too-tight bodice.

Because this wasn't part of their deal, was it? They weren't supposed to be doing this.

'Zayed,' she said desperately, shivering with longing as the mattress dipped beneath his weight and suddenly he was lying next to her, stroking his thumb reflectively over the silky black fabric of her gown and making her nipple grow hard. She tried to hold back her instinctive cry of pleasure. 'We...we mustn't.'

'Mustn't what?'

He stroked some more and made her squirm and although it was as much as she could do to keep her eyes open, she forced herself to meet the mockery in his gaze.

'We're not...we're not allowed to have sex. You know that,' she gasped, because now he was rucking the delicate fabric of her dress up her legs, all the way to her panties and her thighs were weak and trembling. 'We're not supposed to be...' she struggled to get the words out but it was difficult when his hand was on her leg like that '...*consummating* our marriage!'

'And we're not going to.'

'Then what...?' She shuddered again as he began to circle his finger around one of her stocking tops. 'What do you think you're doing?'

'Why don't you let me take care of this?' he said unevenly.

'Take care of what?'

'We're allowed to have pleasure, surely? Just not full, penetrative sex.' His voice grew husky as he continued to explore the band of delicate lace around her thigh. 'But there are plenty of other things we can do which don't cross that particular barrier.'

Jane swallowed, some warning bell in her befuddled brain telling her this wasn't right but the sensations which were shooting through her body were making objection impossible. 'Are you sure that's… allowed?'

'If the King decrees it, then it is allowed.'

'How very arrogant,' she breathed.

'I never claimed not to be arrogant. Just as I never promised not to bend the rules to suit our needs.' He touched his lips to hers so she could feel the warmth of his breath on her lips. 'We'll be sticking to the spirit of the law, if not exactly the letter.'

'Zayed…' Her throat now felt so thick that she could barely get the word out, especially as his finger had left her stocking top and was slowly inching towards her panties.

'Don't you want to have an orgasm, Jane?' he questioned idly. 'To come beneath my fingers and experience a bliss like no other?'

Her mouth dried and she licked her lips as she felt his fingertip brushing over the taut, damp fabric. 'I—'

'You've read all those erotic Kafalahian texts,

haven't you?' he said. 'I know you have, because I've seen them open in that book beside the bed. You've seen all those different acts of pleasure which are possible between a man and a woman. You know very well that fulfilment can be attained through use of the fingers, the mouth and the tongue. It's not all about the penis, Jane.'

'Zayed!' she remonstrated, colour flooding into her cheeks because nobody had ever said that word to her before. *Nobody.*

'Haven't you ever thought that you might like to try some of those techniques yourself?' he persisted softly—now stroking his finger up and down the centre panel of her panties.

Of course she had. But that was a bit like someone stuck in a land-locked country imagining what it would be like to go swimming in the sea every morning. She'd just never associated it with her. She was stolid Jane and serious Jane, but never sexy Jane. Or at least, she hadn't been. Until now. Now she was feeling very sexy indeed and it was all down to this man.

He edged his fingertip beneath the elastic of her panties and she shuddered as she felt his fingers touch the acutely sensitive flesh which was growing wetter by the second. 'Zayed,' she said faintly as she squirmed with pleasure.

'Do you want that, Jane? Only I need you to tell

me,' he murmured. 'I promise I won't do anything to you unless I have your consent.'

And in that moment she hated him for his need to control and for his desire to have her capitulate when he must have known she could no more have stopped what he was doing than she could have grown wings and soared high up to the ceiling of the ambassadorial suite.

'Yes,' she gasped.

'You want me to make you come?'

'Yes! I want you to make me come. Just do it, will you, Zayed? Please.'

She could scarcely believe she'd been so bold but he stopped his teasing then. The playfulness was replaced by a brief shuttering of his eyes, as if the control which was so much a part of him was in danger of slipping away. But when he opened them again all that control was back. His mouth was hard and determined as he shifted his position slightly. Slithering her panties down over her knees and ankles, he tossed them aside before sliding his hand between her thighs once more and lowering his head to kiss her. And Jane moaned with pleasure because it was a double onslaught—the touch of his lips on her mouth and the touch of his fingers on the most intimate part of her was threatening to send her out of her mind.

Her thighs parted as he tangled his nails in the soft fuzz of hair there, before his finger dipped deeper to explore her heated flesh. He kissed away her mounting cries as he strummed against her with a practised touch and she could feel her fingernails digging convulsively into the fabric of his suit jacket. And when it happened it took her by surprise—a great whooshing feeling which gathered her up like a rising wave, before dashing her back down to a heavenly place as spasms racked her body and she said his name, over and over again.

Some time later—she wasn't sure how much because time seemed to have slowed and entered a completely different dimension—she came back down to earth. Her fingers had somehow burrowed inside his suit jacket and she was nestled up close to his chest, like an abandoned kitten who'd unexpectedly been given warmth and shelter. As if she'd found her own little portion of paradise. She could hear the beat of his heart against her ear and it felt as though up until that moment she'd only ever been a shadow of the person she was meant to be. As if a whole new Jane had emerged into a world where everything seemed different. She opened her eyes and looked around. The colours in the room looked more intense. The ticking of the grandfather clock sounded like music to her ears. But when she glanced across at him, she saw he was staring at the ceiling, his profile like granite.

'Zayed?' she said hesitantly.

He turned his head to look at her but she could read nothing in the blackness of his eyes.

'Better?'

His words were a shock—no doubt about it—and her intense feelings of pleasure began to shut down. He'd made what had just happened sound like an itch she'd needed to scratch, or a hunger she'd had to feed. Was that how he saw it—as nothing but a very physical response?

And what if he did?

This wasn't real, she reminded herself fiercely. Did she really want him murmuring meaningless words of affection which would fill her with a hope she had no right to feel? No, she did not. There was nothing wrong with experiencing pleasure for pleasure's sake and she would match his attitude with a coolness of her own.

Stretching her arms above her head, she knew she wasn't imagining the watchful flicker in his eyes but now wasn't the time to give into the stupid urge which was making her long to shower his hawkish face with a million soft, little kisses. Because that was nothing but a hormonal reaction to what had just happened—the logical side of her brain knew that.

'Much better,' she agreed.

'Your first orgasm,' he observed.

'Indeed.'

He looked slightly taken aback, as if her reaction wasn't quite what he'd been expecting. Was that what renewed the sudden spark of fire in his eyes? He turned onto his side, a smile playing at the edges of his lips as he took her hand in his and kissed each finger in turn.

'Purely in the interests of fairness,' he continued softly, 'don't you think I should teach you how to pleasure me in return?'

It was a question which would have shocked her profoundly just a few short weeks ago, but it shocked her no longer. Jane stared into the gleam of his jet-dark eyes. She wanted a sexual education, yes. She wanted to learn all about her body and what it was capable of and learning had always been the thing she was best at. But for once in her life it was difficult to be objective. Difficult not to give into the desire to trace a finger over his lips and tell him he was the most beautiful man she'd ever seen.

But she knew that unwanted affection would serve no purpose in this very functional marriage of theirs. Wasn't it vital to keep emotion out of it? Composing her face into an expression of neutrality, Jane smiled.

'I think that sounds like a very sensible suggestion,' she said, in the same kind of voice she might have used if he'd asked her to pull out a reference book from the library.

CHAPTER NINE

IT SHOULD HAVE been enough. More than enough. And yet it was not nearly enough. Zayed found himself feeling intensely frustrated, despite pleasuring and being pleasured by his virginal wife whenever there was a window of opportunity. He taught the earnest Jane everything he knew as well as stuff he'd never tried—because stopping short of actual consummation meant his imagination needed to be engaged as never before. During long and inventive encounters in their marital quarters of the Kafalahian palace, he discovered a whole new definition of sensuality.

He'd never had to hold back like this before, nor to temper his desire. Women were always instantly compliant when they were with him. They always told him they wanted to feel him *inside them* and the feeling had been mutual. He'd certainly never been made to wait for anything before.

'Not even when you were a teenager?' asked Jane curiously.

They were lying on top of the bed, while the desert sun streamed in through the unshuttered windows in great shafts of gold.

'No.' He shook his head. 'Women always gave themselves completely to me, right from the start.'

'So you never tried *frottage* before?'

'Jane,' he murmured as he remembered the way she'd just been rubbing her fully clothed body against his and his groin hardened as he recalled the intense orgasm which had followed. 'How can someone as innocent as you talk about *frottage* so uninhibitedly—and how do you manage to be so damned good at everything you try, when it's all brand-new to you?'

'Because I'm an academic,' she said. 'Which means I have a need to use the correct terminology for what we've been doing. As well as an enquiring and open mind, which enables me to research and excel in the subject of my choice. And that's what I've been doing.' She stroked her hand over his thigh. 'Haven't I?'

'Jane.' Zayed closed his eyes and groaned. 'By all the stars in the night-time heavens, will you please stop?'

Her hand stilled.

'Is that what you want me to do?' she whispered.

'Yes. No. *Hell!*' He sucked in a ragged breath because the truth was he didn't know *what* he wanted any more. His clever wife had captivated him and kept him guessing, while demonstrating a vivid sexual imagination which took his breath away. Even the intense debate in the international press which had followed the news of his grandfather's surprising bequest had failed to engage him, because all he could think about was Jane. Jane, who had blossomed beneath his daily tutoring. Jane, who had learned her lessons all too well.

He felt her fingers inch their way a little further and his erection grew almost unbearable. 'I was planning to go and inspect my new brood mare,' he growled.

She appeared to give this some consideration for her fingers slowed just long enough to frustrate the hell out of him. 'Okay,' she said lightly. 'I'll see you later.'

Why wasn't she begging him to stay? Why was she about to sit up as if to take her leave of him? Why was she so *headstrong* beneath that calm and sensible exterior?

'No,' he growled. 'Stay. Stay and bring me pleasure.' He pulled her back towards him and expelled a pent-up breath as her hand resumed its journey, beginning to stroke reflectively at a thigh which had tensed with longing.

She bent her head to brush a kiss over his lips. 'I thought you might value a little more down time. You've been working very hard since we got back from Washington.'

He opened his mouth to say something, but whatever he was about to say was forgotten because by now she was pushing aside his silken robes and not for the first time he cursed the fact he wasn't wearing western clothes, because at least they provided a kind of natural barrier to these encounters. It was easier to stop a woman when zips and buttons and the unyielding nature of suit trousers got in the way. But when all that lay between you and a determined hand were several filmy layers of robe—what chance did a man have? He felt as if he were being caught inside a silken web, with no immediate means of escape. As if she were binding him tighter with each intricate strand she wove. *And wasn't the truth that sometimes he felt himself resenting it? Hating the fact that she seemed to be so in control of her emotions, when women usually were not?*

She began to lick his balls, concentrating on each one with a soft kind of intensity, as if she were working her way through an ice cream and trying to make it last as long as possible. Zayed sucked in a hot breath as he held back another groan, unwilling to distract her from her erotic task. His hands tensed like the claws of a falcon as the fabric was pushed to his waist and cool air rushed over his groin. Golden-brown hair fanned over his belly as she slid her fingers over his rigid shaft, her eyes glancing up to meet his gaze as slowly she began to lower her lips onto it. He held his breath, terrified she was going to stop, even though he knew she wouldn't. Each movement of her head took him deeper into her mouth until he felt he was drowning in pleasure. Once again he tried to control his reaction—holding off for as long as possible until a sudden maverick flicker of her tongue was his downfall and his fingers held onto her head as he jerked his seed helplessly inside her mouth.

Afterwards he slumped back, his throat dry and his brow damp with sweat as his heart beat out a primitive tattoo.

'This is driving me crazy,' he growled. 'You are driving me crazy.'

She kissed his bare stomach and looked up. 'You're not complaining, are you, Zayed? You've just had an orgasm. And a very satisfying orgasm, judging by your reaction.'

'That isn't the point.'

'Really? Then I must be missing something. I thought that was the whole point of sex—other than procreation, of course, and obviously we're not going *there*.' She pushed her mussed hair back from her face. 'In fact, it might interest you to know that one of your ancestors once wrote in his diary that he preferred members of his harem to administer oral sex because it meant he didn't have to exert himself in any way—which proved especially valuable in the desert heat, in the days before air-conditioning—'

'I don't give a damn what my ancestors said!'

'No?' She looked at him, her eyebrows slightly raised, and he was reminded of her expression during those usually frosty encounters when she'd been working at the embassy and he'd been there on official business. His eyes narrowed. What had happened to the woman she'd been then? The woman in the shapeless clothes with her hair scraped back into a tight bun. Had this deeply sensual side always been there—just waiting for a desert sheikh to liberate it? Or would the tall geek from the Foreign Office have managed to produce the same reaction? Zayed felt his body tense.

'No,' he bit out. 'I don't.'

'So why are you in such a grumpy mood? What's your problem?' she questioned.

She was. She was his problem, and he couldn't work out why. She was being the best wife she could be in the circumstances—considering he didn't actually *want* a wife. She hadn't tried to rehash all the things he'd confided in her. There had been no more probing questions, nor attempts to delve further into his painful past. She hadn't preened with pride because she'd been the sole recipient of his confidences.

She was discreet, he realised—yet another attribute which had made her so good at her job—but that very discretion was frustrating. He'd told her he didn't want to talk any more about his past but he'd expected her to at least *try*.

So that he could rebuff her attempts to get underneath his skin and push her further away from him?

Probably.

The trouble was that she seemed to be binding herself closer without appearing to do *anything*. He told himself that her appeal lay solely in the fact that she was forbidden to him—and he was a man who had always chased the forbidden. *That* was what made her so fascinating.

'Come here,' he said, lifting her so that she was lying on top of him, belly to belly and groin to groin, and he saw her eyes darken, though a faint frown appeared on her brow.

'Be careful,' she said as his fingers slipped beneath her robe.

'No need to worry,' he said. 'You're wearing panties, aren't you?'

Her cheeks went pink. 'You do say the most outrageous things sometimes.'

She was such a delicious contrast, he thought. So prim and the proper and yet underneath it all— she had a wild sexual appetite which only he had untapped. Instantly he could feel himself growing hard again and so, judging by the widening of her eyes, did she. He wondered what she would do if he pushed her panties aside and eased slowly inside her, like two teenagers who could hold back no longer—a state of affairs which had never applied to him because his lovers had always given him exactly what he wanted. But wasn't that what he felt like now—a teenage boy with little experience, out of his depth in a situation which seemed to have developed a life of its own? He met her gaze and acknowledged the deepening heat which had flared over her cheeks. 'Wouldn't it be so easy?' he questioned. 'To just do it?'

Wriggling away from his grasp, she quickly got up from the bed and smoothed down her tunic. 'And then what? All this would have been in vain. The marriage would then have been consummated and we wouldn't be able to get it annulled.'

'Nobody would know,' he continued reflectively. 'I have looked in the statute books and discovered that non-consummation is unbelievably difficult to prove.'

'But we would know,' she said reprovingly and then something seemed to change on her face as she went to stand by the window to gaze out at the desert sky. 'I think I would find it difficult to live with that level of deceit, Zayed. And we'd be running the risk of perjuring ourselves, which I can't honestly believe you would be prepared to do.'

He gave a heavy sigh. Why did she always have to be so damned *right*? 'No,' he said slowly. 'I guess not.'

Her shoulders were stiff with tension and he found himself wanting to ask what was going on in that head of hers and this frustrated him too, because asking a woman what she was thinking was surely the beginning of the end! 'Jane?' he said meditatively.

But Jane wasn't really listening. She was wondering how much longer she could maintain this façade of pretending she had no real feelings about the man she'd married, of acting as though all this meant nothing. Pretending that she cared about nothing but having orgasms when inside her heart was becoming ensnared by Zayed with each sweet kiss he gave her.

Outside their bedroom window the sky was as blue as the party dress her mother had bought Cleo all those years ago, but inside Jane's heart felt darker than it had done when she'd unwrapped her own dress to discover it was a dull and sensible navy. Her mother hadn't intended to be cruel—she had simply been acknowledging the differences between her two daughters, one so pretty and the other so practical. And nothing had really changed. She needed to remember that. She was still practical Jane and beneath all her royal finery she was plain Jane, too. A few dazzling jewels and a title didn't actually change that.

She had Zayed's interest now, but it wouldn't last. It couldn't. He was fascinated by her, yes—even she with her lack of experience could tell that—but only because she remained elusive. She knew that sometimes he watched her when she wasn't looking, just as she knew he often smiled at some of the things she said—and he wasn't a man prone to giving many smiles. But he didn't know the truth, did he? He had no idea she was trying very hard not to be the Jane she had become... The woman who wanted to melt whenever he kissed her. Who hungered to feel him deep inside her, instead of their controlled and ultimately shallow methods of achieving pleasure. Who longed to carry his child with a passion which startled her.

Because somewhere along the way she'd come to know the man beneath the arrogant exterior. To understand him better and to *like* him. And that liking was in danger of tipping into loving. Loving someone who didn't want her love—a damaged man who hid his pain well beneath his success and his swagger. There had been no more bad dreams since he'd told her about what had happened to his mother and he'd never mentioned that painful subject again. She couldn't deny the satisfaction it gave her to think that she might have helped liberate him from some of his demons. But she shouldn't take that satisfaction and try to turn it into something it could never be.

And wouldn't Zayed run a million miles if he guessed what her true feelings were? If he realised that some nights she lay awake wondering how she was going to endure the next few months with him, despite the mutual pleasure they gave each other. Terrified that she was going to reveal herself with a candid word or a slip of the tongue. She thought about the country she had hungered all her adult life to see—and how ironic it was that she spent an inordinate amount of time in their bedroom, despite having been given complete access to all the palace artefacts and its magnificent library.

'Will I get to see Qaiyama before I leave?' she questioned suddenly.

'We have months to think about that.'

'I know we do, but I'd like to go before winter sets in. I've heard over the last few years it's been snowing in the region and cutting off the city.' She turned to face him. 'Is that possible, do you think?'

An arrogant smile touched the edges of his lips. 'Anything is possible for your Sheikh, Jane. You have only to ask.'

She wanted to correct him but for once she didn't bother. Because these weren't academic matters she was dealing with—straightforward facts which could be verified or negated. Matters of the heart didn't conform to any particular set of rules, she was discovering. Of course not *everything* was possible for

Zayed—it wasn't possible he could ever love her, was it?

They planned their trip for the end of the following week, travelling across the vast reaches of the country by one of the royal aircraft. Before she left, Jane sent an email to David Travers, enquiring tentatively about possible openings within the Foreign Office. Because she had to start looking to her future. She knew that when this was over she couldn't return to her old job. How would it look to have the newly divorced Sheikha back in her basement office, wading through dusty reams of documents? Apart from anything else, what would happen when Zayed came to visit? Would she have to pretend that they'd been nothing to one another—or, worse still, to remember exactly what they'd done, and how?

She hadn't received a reply from David by the time they touched down and she forgot all about it in the light of the surprise which was awaiting her. Jane had been expecting to be taken straight to the city, but instead they had landed in the vast emptiness of the desert. She blinked. Well, not completely empty because before her loomed a vast tent—with a group of other, smaller tents in the distance. Against the flaming splendour of the sunset rose a pyramid-shaped roof and through the open flaps of the entrance to the main tent she could see the faint gleam of embellished wall-hangings.

She turned to Zayed. 'What...what is this?'

'Surely you recognise a Bedouin tent?' he questioned mockingly. 'Did you not once tell me that your heart's desire was to stay in one?'

Yes, she had said that. Soft words of longing which she'd confided to him during those early days of sexual discovery, when she had been able to enjoy pleasure for pleasure's sake—before the unrealistic demands of her heart had made her want so much more. She could hardly turn to him now, could she, and voice her concerns that the sheer romance of the setting would cause her unnecessary pain? So she followed her husband into the interior, where lavish wrought-iron lamps hung from the canvas ceiling and cast a golden glow. Priceless silk carpets adorned the floor and low divans were covered in rich and heavy brocade.

'One of the maidservants will take you away to be bathed,' said Zayed softly, and, as if she'd heard his words, a young woman appeared in the doorway.

Jane wanted to protest as she was led away to where a bath had been prepared for her. How on earth had they managed to produce this much warm water in the middle of the desert? she wondered as she lowered her body into the milky depths. But for once her questioning mind was silenced by the delicious sensation of the scented oils rippling over her. Afterwards, the maidservant rubbed the silkiest cream into her skin, so that she smelt the drift of sweet oranges and bergamot as she was helped into her clothes. And what clothes. She'd never seen these silk-chiffon robes before and they were the most exquisite thing she'd ever laid eyes on. In deep indigo—as rich and as dark as the desert sky—the robes were delicately embroidered with silver and studded with tiny gems which glittered as she moved, so that she felt as if she were wearing the night sky wrapped around her.

Her hair was left loose and she made her way towards the main tent beneath a sky dazzling with a blaze of stars and the perfect shining scimitar of a golden moon. This must be what it had been like for his ancestors, she thought suddenly. Because out here in the beautiful starkness of the desert, nothing had really changed. Inside the tent the overhead lights had been extinguished and in their place were dozens of candles, which reinforced the fairytale feel. As Zayed heard her enter and turned to greet her Jane thought she would recall that look on his face for as long as she lived. Or would she try to forget it on the grounds that it would be too achingly poignant to remember? For in that unguarded moment she saw desire, yes, but wasn't there something else flickering in his black eyes? Some other emotion which looked like a deeper kind of longing than mere lust.

Maybe she was just guilty of transferring her own

feelings onto him. Imagining what she *wanted* to see instead of what was really there.

'You like it?' she questioned, only her voice did not sound like her voice at all. It sounded husky and tremulous.

'I…' He hesitated and that in itself was rare. 'I have never seen a woman more beautiful than the way you look tonight, my Queen.'

She wanted to tell him not to talk to her that way and yet she wanted him never to stop. She was glad to take the weight off her trembling knees and to sink onto the embroidered cushions which were heaped in front of the traditional low table. The Sheikh's favoured foods were brought to them on golden platters, accompanied by the sweet date juice for which the region was famous. But Jane could barely concentrate on the delicacies on offer; she was much too churned up inside to eat or drink. And when the barely touched dishes were taken away, Zayed took her into his arms, smoothing the hair back from her cheeks with his fingers.

'So pensive tonight, Jane.'

She shrugged. 'This is quite some experience.' She looked around the room, desperately seeking to focus her attention on something other than the burning temptation of his eyes. 'For once I find myself lost for words.'

But he turned her face back to his, his palm cupping her chin so she could look nowhere else but at him. 'Then perhaps we should occupy ourselves with something which requires no words.'

He kissed her and it should have been wonderful—and in a way Jane supposed it was. They both achieved orgasm that night, didn't they? Not just once but over and over. He caressed her with his mouth and with his hands. He explored every aching centimetre of skin until she was crying out yet again beneath the renewed heat of desire. But never had Jane been more aware of the shallow nature of their relationship and the fact that they weren't giving themselves to each other as fully as they could. Because he didn't want to. Because she wasn't supposed to be his real *lover*. She was his convenient wife, that was all, and for only a limited tenure.

Here in the romantic setting of the Bedouin tent it was easy to forget the harshness of their reality and allow herself to be swept away by the fantasy of imagining him as her *real* husband. And she mustn't let herself. As she lay in the stillness of the desert night, listening to the sound of Zayed's steady breathing, she tried to concentrate on her gratitude that he no longer suffered those terrible nightmares. And with an effort she pushed away her growing sense of hopelessness for what could never be.

Despite the matchless beauty and solitude of the place, Jane felt a sense of relief when they left by plane the following morning to install themselves in Zayed's sumptuous palace in Qaiyama. And she was glad of the opportunity to distract herself from her uncomfortable thoughts by exploring the city which had once been Kafalah's capital. With its bustling bazaars, enormous square and the famous clock tower which overlooked the ancient temple, it was still very romantic—but in a much more manageable way than the Bedouin tent had been. She had a million questions for their learned guide, most of which he was able to answer but there were a couple which he confessed perplexed him. Jane said she would research the answers herself and let him know, and she saw the curving smile on Zayed's face as he listened.

She was hot and dusty by the time they returned to the palace and made a couple of quick notes on her computer before going into the bathroom to douse her hot skin with the refreshing splash of a cool shower. It wasn't nearly as relaxing as bathing by candlelight in the desert, but she reflected that you couldn't have everything. Her hair was damp and her silk robe brushing against her scented skin when she walked back into the room and saw something on Zayed's face that she'd never seen there before. She frowned, her senses instantly alert. Something she couldn't quite put her finger on.

What was it?

'Everything okay?' she questioned.

'Couldn't be better.' He began to walk towards her. 'Did you see how much pleasure you gave to our guide today, when he realised that the new Queen was so literate in Kafalahian history?'

She was about to make a flippant remark about enjoying being a queen while it lasted, but something in Zayed's eyes stopped her. Something dark and dangerous. But dangerous in an exciting way, if that was possible. Her tongue snaked out to moisten her suddenly dry lips. 'Is…is something the matter?' she said.

'The matter?' His hand reached out to cup her face and she could feel the roughness of his fingers as they smoothed over her skin and it matched the sudden roughness of his voice. 'On the contrary, I'm just beginning to realise what a fool I've been, Jane.'

'You? A fool?'

'Mmm. I know it is difficult to comprehend, but even I am capable of making fundamental mistakes.'

Curiosity overrode her desire to reproach him for coming out with such an arrogant statement. 'What sort of mistakes?'

He pulled her into his arms and brushed his lips over hers. 'I want to possess you so much that it's eating me up,' he husked. 'I can't go on like this for much longer, Jane—and, what's more, I don't intend to try.'

Her heart was beating so fast that she could hardly speak. She assumed he was just going to pleasure her in one of the usual ways but suddenly there was a new tension about him which told her something had changed. 'Do you want me to try to work out what you mean from the vague clues you're giving me?'

He gave a laugh. A soft laugh edged with mockery but tinged with something darker. 'Ah, Jane,' he murmured. 'Clever, clever Jane. I don't doubt for a moment that you could work out my meaning if I gave you enough clues, but that would only waste precious time and I'm not prepared to waste any more.'

'I don't understand.'

'But you will. Very soon you will,' he promised as he stroked a reflective fingertip over her trembling lip. 'I'm going to make love to you. Fully. Properly. Completely.'

'But we c—'

'Yes, we can,' he intervened, and before she had a chance to protest any further his other hand started caressing the indentation of her waist through the soft silk of her gown. 'I have spoken to my lawyers.'

'Lawyers?' she repeated faintly, because, in the context of his hands smoothing down over her body, the word seemed to jar.

'Mmm.' His lips were on her neck now. 'The conditions of the will have been met and I have inherited Dahabi Makaan. It is done. So now we can do the hell what we want.'

'But that means we won't be able to dissolve the

marriage within six months!' she said, trying desperately to ignore the thundering of her heart and sudden rush of heat to her sex. 'We'll have to wait at least two years for a separation.'

'And would that bother you?' he questioned, his fingers splaying over one engorged breast.

At that moment she was so aroused that she felt the whole Kafalahian army could have charged through their bedroom and it wouldn't have bothered her. Because six months or two years—what difference would it make? They were still going to get divorced, weren't they? *And why shouldn't Zayed be the man to take her virginity when she wanted him so much? Why shouldn't she enjoy that unique and precious experience with someone she'd come to care for more deeply than she'd ever imagined?*

'I guess I could live with that,' she said coolly, determined not to scare him away with her eagerness.

'Then so be it.'

His lips were no longer on her throat and his voice was no longer a murmur. It had the undeniable ring of determination, which matched the darkening of his face as he picked her up and carried her over to the divan like every masterful fantasy she'd ever had about him. By time he peeled the robe from her body she was already desperate and aching as she watched him undress. She was scared and excited as all that magnificent tawny flesh was revealed, her hungry gaze taking in the broad shoulders, the narrowed hips and the powerful shafts of his muscular legs. And there, at the cradle of his groin, was the daunting sight of his erection—so big and so proud. She had touched him there so many times before but now—at last—she was going to feel him deep inside her.

He came to lie on the divan beside her, his finger tracing light circles around each of her puckered nipples, before bending his head to lick each one in turn and Jane shivered as tremors of pure bliss rippled over her. She'd thought that once the decision had been made Zayed would seek to possess her very quickly but to her surprise he seemed to be taking all the time in the world. How could he be so controlled, she wondered yearningly, when it was plain that he was as tense and as hungry as she? She sucked in a ragged breath as his tongue cleaved its way over her belly while his fingers moved against her heated sex.

'How long shall I make you wait?' he questioned, almost idly. 'Long enough to make you beg, as you begged me that first time I ever touched you intimately?'

'Is that what you want?' she gasped, but he shook his head.

'You can never give me what I want, Jane,' he answered, his voice dark. 'But I can give you what *you* want. And I can ensure that you will never forget me for as long as you draw breath. That no man will ever come close to giving you the pleasure which you are about to experience in my arms.'

It had the ring of a territorial boast and something about the dark note underpinning it told Jane she ought to stop him, because their needs were too different. She cared for him more than he cared for her. More than she suspected he would be capable of caring—for anyone. She bit her lip, knowing that everything he'd said had been true. If she let him take her virginity, she would never be able to rid herself of his memory—his hawkish face and hard body would haunt her for as long as she lived. But she couldn't stop him. She couldn't and, what was more, she didn't want to. So instead she just lay there as his gaze was directed to the swell of her rapidly rising breasts before travelling down to stare at the soft triangle of hair between her thighs. It was a candidly assessing look and for a moment she could imagine what a whore must feel like, but somehow she didn't care about that either.

'You have one last chance to change your mind,' he said softly, as if he'd been able to read her thoughts.

She shook her head. 'I don't want to change my mind.'

He smiled as he moved over her and parted her thighs and she could feel the tip of his erection teasing her moist flesh. And although they had come this far before, this time was different. His eyes were dark with ebony fire as he looked straight into hers and slowly entered her.

It hurt, yes—but only a little—and the hurt was quickly replaced by an indescribable feeling of warmth and joy because this was what she had wanted for so long. He filled her and she cried out his name. He pushed deeper inside her and she said his name again. And again. Wrapping her legs around his back, Jane gave herself up to the delicious rhythm as he began to move, her hands at his shoulders and her lips at his neck. She gasped as she felt her orgasm building and the familiar pleasure began to sweep her up—and suddenly she was crying out loud and so was he. As the delicious spasms racked her body he gave a low, shuddering moan as he bucked inside her.

For a while they said nothing. Feeling closer to him than she'd ever done before, Jane tightened her arms around him as she lay listening to the muffled thud of his slowing heart, wanting nothing more than to just savour the moment. But somehow she couldn't hold back the unwanted thoughts which came flooding into her mind. She wasn't unrealistic enough to hope for words of love but wasn't it possible that they needn't rush into getting a divorce? That Zayed might be prepared to give their marriage a chance?

'That probably wasn't the smartest move in the world,' he drawled.

His words startled her and, uncomprehendingly, Jane raised her head to stare at him. 'I'm sorry?'

Shaking his dark head, he withdrew from her. 'We shouldn't have done that.'

'Well, I know.' She swallowed. 'But we did.'

'Yes, we did,' he agreed, his hawkish face tight with tension. 'Maybe it was inevitable after all these weeks. Unrealistic of me to think I could share my bed with a woman and not possess her.'

Suddenly Jane wanted to scream. She'd thought it had been about passion but for Zayed it seemed to have been all about possession.

'I've let you down,' he continued, still in that same tight tone. 'And because of that I'm going to let you go.'

'Let me go?' she repeated, because wasn't that the euphemism bosses used when they wanted to sack someone?

'I've broken my word—something I've never done before,' he said, and suddenly she could see contempt contorting his tawny features. 'So I'm setting you free, Jane. I'm not going to mess you around more than I already have done. I don't need you. Not any more. I've done what I set out to do and done what I needed to do for my people. You can walk away from me right now.'

She opened her mouth to say she didn't want to walk away until she realised it wasn't an option. This was the Sheikh's command, thinly disguised as concern for *her* welfare. Was she going to humiliate herself by begging him yet again?

Stiffly she got up, picking up her discarded robe from the floor and pulling it over her head, relieved to disguise her nakedness from his piercing gaze. 'In that case, can you organise my return to England as quickly as possible?' she questioned, her voice low and shaking.

He sat up, the rumpled golden sheet falling to his waist. 'Have you got enough money?'

'We agreed my fee at the very beginning, if you remember,' she answered coolly and then curiosity got the better of her. She remembered the darkness on his face as he'd started to seduce her. She remembered the harshness which had underpinned his words just before he had entered her.

'Something has changed, hasn't it?' she said slowly. 'Something which made you want to break your word and have sex with me. It wasn't just because you'd cleared your inheritance with your lawyers, was it, Zayed? It was something else.'

He gave a hard smile as he pushed back the rumpled sheet and pulled on his own robe. 'I think you know the answer to that yourself, Jane.'

'Actually, no. I don't have a clue what you're talking about.'

'Really?' He stood up and there was a pause as

his gaze skated over her. 'You haven't been secretly writing to lover-boy from the Foreign Office, then?'

It took a full ten seconds before she realised what he was talking about. 'You've bēen reading my emails!' she said in a low voice. 'You've been *spying* on me!'

'The computer was open on the desk,' he snapped. 'When a message came through while you were in the shower, I didn't realise it was open on your account. And it was from *David*. How touching. Nice of him to be planning a cosy new beginning for you for when you start your new life. You didn't waste much time, did you?'

She met his eyes. 'Why exactly did you just have sex with me, Zayed?' she questioned. 'Just tell me the truth. Please. That's all I ask.'

There was a pause and she saw something like indecision shadow his features. A split second of hesitation, as if he recognised that there could be no coming back from what he was about to say.

'Because I imagined you in the arms of David Travers and I couldn't bear the thought of another man being the first.'

And that was the moment she knew it really was over. It had been all about possession, not passion—she had been right all along.

She pushed a wayward lock of hair back from her face. 'I'd like to leave as soon as possible.'

'Where are you going to go?'

Jane realised he didn't actually *care* about her answer—he was simply protecting his precious reputation, probably thinking that it wouldn't look good if the estranged wife of the Sheikh was going off to live somewhere unsuitable. Because he had shut down emotionally, she realised. He'd gone back to being the Zayed he preferred to be. They'd just had full sex but they might as well not have bothered. At the time she'd felt close to him but the feeling obviously hadn't been reciprocated. All she represented to him now was a symbol of his failure to resist her, and she suspected he would never forgive himself for that. Or her.

So she gave him a cool smile. The kind of smile intended to let him know that this really was the end of their ill-fated marriage. That once she walked out of that door there would be no coming back. Her heart felt shattered enough as it was—there was no way she was going to risk inflicting any further pain on it.

'Where I'm going is none of your business, Zayed. This is it. It's over. I don't want anything more to do with you,' she said quietly. And, walking into the adjoining bathroom, she locked the door behind her.

CHAPTER TEN

FOR THE FIRST time in her life, Jane was without a plan. Within hours she had left Kafalah and flown into London, but she didn't go back to her half of her rented house. She didn't dare. She'd told Zayed she wanted nothing more to do with him, but she was aware that nothing was that straightforward. For the time being she was still legally his wife. What if he decided on a whim that he wanted some more hot sex with her? He might try to seek her out to do just that and she wasn't going to risk it.

She didn't dare risk being unable to resist him.

So, dreading what she might find when she got there, she travelled to Cleo's home, surprised to discover that her sister had moved. No longer in a scruffy room in the farthest outreaches of East London, her twin was now ensconced in Ascot, in a cute little cottage which stood in the grounds of an enormous mansion.

'I'm a housekeeper,' said Cleo, by way of explanation. 'And don't look so surprised, Jane. Did you really think I was going to live in a shoebox for the rest of my life, trying and failing to be a model?' Her gaze had narrowed. 'Didn't you ever think I might be capable of turning things around—or is it only you who is capable of positive change?'

'No, of course not,' said Jane slowly as she put her single suitcase in the hallway, thinking how badly wrong her sister had got it because nothing *positive* had come out of her ill-fated marriage to Zayed. Nothing but an ache deep in her heart and a sense of how badly she was going to miss him. 'It's just I can't imagine you as a housekeeper.'

Cleo smiled. 'Being subservient, you mean—on my knees, scrubbing floors, like Cinderella? You don't *honestly* think I'd risk ruining my manicure?' She wiggled her bright red fingernails in the air. 'No danger of that! The guy who owns it is some big-shot billionaire who's never around, who employs an army of cleaners and gardeners to look after the main house. I just live there when he's away and my presence is supposed to deter any would-be burglars.'

'But is it safe?' questioned Jane worriedly.

'I told him I had a black belt in judo.'

'Oh, Cleo—you didn't?'

'Why not? I am actually learning at evening class, so who knows? And anyway.' Cleo was looking at her thoughtfully. 'That's enough about me. Are you going to tell me why you've been crying?'

'I haven't been crying.'

'Jane,' said her sister gently. 'This is me, remember? I know you and I can hardly believe the state of you. You *never* cry.'

The trouble was that ever since she'd left Kafalah she couldn't seem to stop. Tears began to well up in her eyes as she sank onto a sofa while Cleo made her a cup of tea she didn't really want. And suddenly Jane was glad she'd never had a relationship before now, or had her heart broken. Why had nobody told her it would feel like *this*?

'Okay,' said Cleo solemnly as she sat down on the sofa next to her. 'The last I heard, you were whooping it up in Washington—wowing the locals and having dinner at the White House. What did I miss?'

More tears spilled down her cheeks before Jane dashed them away and the story came tumbling out. Some of it she told how it was, but much of it she missed out. She didn't think anyone had the right to know about someone else's sex-life and even though she was angry with Zayed—angrier than she'd ever been in her entire life—she wasn't going to betray him by talking about the intimacies of what had gone on in their marital bed.

'And then I flew back to England,' she finished, with a sniff.

'Drink your tea.' Cleo handed her the mug. 'So basically, you had a marriage of convenience—the proceeds of which helped bail me out of my predicament and for which I am eternally grateful—and which went wrong when you started to fall in love with him?'

'I never said I was in love with him.'

'Oh, *Jane*. Come on. It's written all over your face.' Cleo's eyes narrowed. 'And he thinks you're interested in this guy David.'

'In a nutshell, yes.'

'But if Zayed doesn't love you...then why was he so jealous of some random guy you knew from college?'

'Because he's possessive,' said Jane darkly. 'He doesn't want me, but he doesn't want anyone else to have me.'

'Masterful,' breathed Cleo admiringly.

'Brutish,' corrected Jane.

'So what are you going to do about it?'

Jane drew in a deep breath as she put down her untouched mug of tea. She'd thought about this until it had spun in an endless cycle around her head. 'I have enough money to live on for the time being,' she said. 'And I'm going to find myself somewhere to live—somewhere cheap and remote—and then I'm going to write the definitive history of Kafalah.'

'But...' Cleo looked slightly confused '...if the

whole point is to forget Zayed, won't writing a book about his country make it impossible?'

Jane shook her head, suddenly fired up by her own resolve. 'It will be cathartic,' she said firmly. 'Nobody's ever done it before, so there's definitely a gap in the market. And it means I can get that wretched country out of my system once and for all,' she finished darkly.

'And what about Zayed? What if he tries to get in touch with you?'

'He won't,' Jane said, hating the instinctive shivering of her skin as she thought of the dark Sheikh turning up on her doorstep out of the blue. 'If he wants to communicate with me, he can do it through his lawyers. His precious lawyers,' she finished bitterly.

In his vast office within the Kafalahian palace, Zayed stared at the painting which hung in pride of place above his desk. A painting not unlike the one he'd donated to his club in London, the one which Jane had recognised on the night he'd taken her to dinner and asked her to become his wife. He looked at the famous three blue towers of Tirabah and realised he'd never once taken her there, so she could see for herself the beautiful vista which so many artists had captured on canvas.

But he didn't want to think about his omissions

as her husband. He wanted to concentrate on her failures as a wife. On the disloyalty she had shown towards him by communicating secretly with another man.

Yet it didn't seem to matter how many times he tried to convince himself otherwise, deep down he was aware that he had behaved very badly towards his English bride. At least, once he'd allowed his jealousy to disperse and started engaging his brain. And when he thought about it properly, he was appalled at how wrong he'd got it. No way would someone like Jane be flirting with some diplomat when it was abundantly clear that she'd made him, Zayed, the focus of her attention. Could he have asked for any more than she had given him? He thought not. Sexually inventive, stimulating company and a huge hit with his court, she had been an exemplary partner in every way.

He shook his head. He had told her he didn't need her any more—just as he'd never needed a mother or father when he was growing up. But no matter how much he tried to convince himself that was true, his arguments sounded increasingly empty. How could he miss her so much? Why did everything seem to lack lustre without her, so that even the gilded fittings of the palace looked dull in the desert sunshine? He stood up and went to the wardrobe where her tunics were still hanging. He knew he should ask one of the staff to remove them and donate them to a worthy cause, but he had been reluctant to do so and he couldn't quite work out why. Was he somehow imagining she might come back? Of course she would never come back—and could he really blame her?

Word had got out, of course, that the Sheikha was no longer in residence. Some of the western press had hinted that all was not well within the marriage and there had been several profile pieces carrying a distinctly disappointed tone that the unusual match hadn't worked out, because the new Queen of the desert had proved to be a big hit in Washington and the rest of the world was eager to meet her.

Zayed's phone had begun to ring—his private line buzzing with calls from ex-lovers casually suggesting hooking up. But their predatory intrusion had made his temper boil and he had instructed Hassan to change his number. Because he didn't want an ex-lover and he didn't want a new lover. He wanted Jane. He realised that when he'd ravished her on the divan he had—for the first time in his life—neglected to wear a condom. Could she be carrying his child? An heir to the throne of Al Zawba? His heart clenched. He had to find out.

But a London aide who was despatched to her home with an armful of flowers was informed that the Queen had moved out and, no, she hadn't left any forwarding address. The news had both infuriated him and excited him, for there was nothing Zayed liked better than a chase. He tried ringing her but it seemed he wasn't the only one who had changed their number. He contacted his embassy in London but nobody had seen or heard from her. He'd even rung a high-powered contact in the Foreign Office who was able to confirm that the Sheikha of Kafalah had *not* applied to enrol on the system's fast-track channel.

And that was when it began to sink in that maybe he had been wrong. Wrong in so many ways. He had judged her by his own standards and done her a terrible disservice. He had treated her as his chattel. He was a brute. Purposefully, he lifted the phone to have one of his planes put on stand-by, planning to make it up to her, knowing there wasn't a woman alive who could resist him when he set his mind to something. After a brief consultation with his aides, he put the journey into motion and within ten hours was touching down at a private airfield just outside London.

But tracking down his wife wasn't as easy as it should have been and he was forced to accept that she didn't want to be found. At least, not by him. It took a great deal of resourcefulness, not to mention a team of private detectives, to determine the whereabouts of Jane's twin sister, Cleo, and when at last he found her, he was surprised. Contrary to what he was expecting, his wife's twin sister was very different from the image he'd formed of her. Despite her dyed blonde hair and eyes the colour of emeralds, she looked a little like Jane. But she was not Jane, he reminded himself bitterly. *She was not Jane.*

And neither was she particularly friendly.

'She doesn't want to see you,' had been her opening gambit.

'I realise that.'

'So what are you doing here?'

Biting back his instinctive retort that nobody should speak to a desert king in such a way, he sucked in a ragged breath instead, telling himself that never had diplomacy been more vital. 'I must see her,' he said simply.

She stared at him very hard for a moment and he didn't know what made her change her mind but at last she grudgingly wrote down Jane's address and phone number and handed it to him.

'All I ask,' said Zayed unsteadily as he glanced down at the information he'd been given, 'is that you don't tell her I'm on my way to see her.'

'Because you know she'd make sure she was out.'

'That's right.' His eyes narrowed. 'Yet you're giving me access to her. Why?'

Cleo hesitated before glaring at him and in that moment he thought she looked *very* like her sister. 'Because this is all such a mess and I don't think she's ever properly going to get over you until she sees you again.'

He nodded. It was not the answer he wanted but at least it was an honest one. 'Thank you.'

Cleo leaned forward, her voice a soft whisper. 'But if you ever hurt her—'

'I promise never to knowingly hurt her,' he said gravely. 'Please believe me when I tell you that.'

His car was waiting in the road outside and he gave the address to the driver, who happened to be English.

'North Wales, Your Royal Highness?' The driver's voice dipped in concern as he stared out at the dark sky. 'Are you sure you wouldn't prefer to set out in the morning? It's a fair old trip in this weather.'

'Now,' said Zayed tersely. 'I want to go there now.'

He'd never been to Wales before, a country he knew was renowned for its beautiful mountains and above average rainfall. It was raining when they passed Birmingham and raining even harder when they drove through a little town called Bala, his bodyguards following at a discreet distance. Finding Jane's cottage wasn't easy because there seemed to be a shortage of signposts, no streetlights, and in the dark and moonless night several sheep suddenly loomed out of the gloom, fixing him with their unwavering stare.

He was wearing jeans, a sweater and a leather

jacket and was glad he'd decided to blend in as much as possible, especially when he walked into a pub which was just closing and the room went silent and everyone stared at him as if he'd just descended from outer space.

He found her place eventually. A tiny cottage joined to several others—just a few yards away from the narrow winding road, with an upstairs window showing a square of golden light. He told the driver to park a little way up, pointing to a nearby layby where he could wait—who knew for how long? And then Zayed got out of the car, sucking in a breath full of cool, damp air as he walked towards the tiny cottage and rapped on the door.

After a couple of minutes, a light went on at the front of the house but he couldn't hear the sound of footfall, only the unbolting of a lock before a pair of shadowed amber eyes peered out at him. In their widening he saw shock and then the glint of fire in their depths. Briefly he thought how immensely flattered any of his other lovers would have been to discover that he had just travelled halfway across the world in order to see them, but on Jane's face there was nothing but hostility.

CHAPTER ELEVEN

FROM INSIDE THE tiny cottage, the knock had sounded authoritative and demanding. Perhaps that was why foreboding had shivered its way down Jane's spine. Or maybe the seemingly habitual cold of her Welsh cottage had seeped beneath her skin and decided to stay there.

She'd tried to tell herself it couldn't be Zayed but who else would be banging on her door at this time of night? She'd been huddled up in bed, trying and failing to get warm while reading about the Kafalah-Hakabar war of 1863. Trying to stop Zayed's hawkish face from swimming into her thoughts and wondering if Cleo had been right all along. That working on a book about his country would make it impossible to forget the current ruler.

Another knock.

Should she ignore it? Hope her silence might make him give up and go away? She sighed, knowing Zayed wasn't the kind of man to give up and go away.

But if she answered it, she couldn't afford to crumble. She needed to stay strong. To remember the way he'd read her emails and accused her of all those outrageous things. To calmly tell him that whatever he said would have no effect on her resolve to put as much distance between them as possible. What she mustn't do was to give any hint of how much she'd been missing him. She was like someone who'd never tasted sugar and then suddenly become addicted to it. At first the sweetness was almost too good to be true…and then too late you discovered it made your teeth rot.

Undoing the chain on the door, she peered out. There were no moon or stars to lighten the night but there was no mistaking the formidable physique silhouetted there, a towering shadow of fathomless black against the darkness.

She kept her voice low. 'What are you doing here?'

His voice was just as soft. 'Maybe I need to know if you're having my baby.'

'Couldn't you have just picked up the phone to ask me that?'

'Are you?'

'No.' Somehow she managed to keep the pain from her voice. To hide the unexpectedness of yet another layer of hurt. 'Whatever else it is you want to say, I don't want to hear it. So why don't you save us both some time and go back where you came from?'

His voice was quiet. 'I'm not going anywhere unless you agree to see me. I'll stand on the doorstep all night until you let me in, if necessary. Alternatively, I could go back to the car to fetch a toolbox and take the door off its hinges.'

'You'll wake the neighbours.'

In the darkness she could see him shrug. 'Then don't make me,' he said.

She expelled an angry sigh. 'You'd better come in.'

He had to dip his head to enter the low-ceilinged cottage and once inside he managed to make everything look as if it were made from cardboard. It was disconcerting to see him in jeans and a leather jacket instead of his usual flowing robes. Somehow it made him resemble some hunk from the poster of an action film and it made him look gloriously and dangerously accessible. She wondered what he thought of *her* get-up—the thick sweater she'd pulled on over her pyjamas and the woolly bed socks which were covering her feet.

But it didn't *matter* what he thought of her appearance. She wasn't trying to impress him, or seduce him. She wasn't even going to ask him to sit down because she wasn't planning on him staying that long.

'So. Why don't you say whatever it is you want to say and then go?'

Zayed nodded as he sucked in a deep breath. He

could feel the blood pounding through his veins and the way his mouth had become as dry as desert dust as he stared into her face. Apology wasn't something which came easily to him for he was a man who found it difficult to accept he'd been in the wrong, but he knew what he needed to say. 'I'm sorry for the way I behaved in Qaiyama.'

She shrugged. 'It was...*regrettable*—but there's nothing we can do about it now. However, thank you for your apology and for the effort you made in coming to give it to me.'

It wasn't what he was expecting but he accepted she was going to make him work a little harder than that. 'But that isn't the only reason I'm here, Jane.'

'Let me guess.' She raised her eyebrows. 'You want to resurrect your ego by demonstrating just how wonderful a lover you can be?'

'While the thought of doing that makes my blood sing,' he said softly, 'what I really want is your forgiveness.'

She shook her head. 'And I don't feel inclined to give it to you,' she said and suddenly she stopped caring about saving face. About pretending not to be hurt. She *was* hurt. That was a fact—and facts were what she dealt with. 'At least, not now. Not yet. Give me a year. Maybe five. Come back when the pain isn't quite so raw and we might even be able to laugh about it.'

'Jane—'

'No,' she said fiercely. 'Whatever it is you want to say, I'm asking you to consider the effect it might have on me first. Please, Zayed. Don't try to seduce me because you want to.' Her voice broke a little. 'Because you can.'

His jaw clenched as she spoke to him, his eyes closing briefly—as if it was rare for someone to heap such censure upon him, and of course it was. But she wasn't here to protect Zayed's feelings…she was too busy trying to safeguard her own.

'I miss you—and that's the truth,' he said, looking straight into her eyes—his gaze direct and dark and unflinching. 'I like having you around, Jane. Much more than I'd realised. I'd never really valued companionship before—I'd always thought it overrated and intrusive—but suddenly I do. I like the way you make me feel and I'm not just talking about sexually. You challenge me intellectually. I've never had that from a woman before. You make me smile and I've never had that before either. You infuriate me with your stubbornness, yet I admire the way you fight your corner. And my people adore you—that is in no doubt. You have the makings of a first-class desert queen, Jane, and I…' He sucked in a deep breath. 'Well, I would like to make the position permanent.'

'You'd like to make the position permanent,' she repeated in a low voice.

'Why not?' He smiled then. That roguish, sexy smile which told her he considered himself on firmer ground now—that he was heading towards the victory of the finishing line as he had done so many times before.

'We have proved our compatibility in many ways,' he continued. 'And I think you're honest enough to admit that you won't ever find another man who compares to me.'

'So you no longer think I was planning to hook up with David Travers as soon as the ink on our divorce papers was dry?'

He shrugged. 'I may have been a little hasty in my judgment.'

'Is that a yes, Zayed?' she persisted. 'Or a no?'

'What is it that you ask of me, Jane?' he demanded. 'When I have given you all that a woman can reasonably expect. I didn't do trust, or confidences or foreplay until I met you and now I realise just how important they are.'

'Just not necessarily in that order, right?'

'Oh, Jane,' he said, frustrated now. 'Do you always have to come up with a clever answer?'

'Why shouldn't I? Hasn't it ever occurred to you that I've had to survive by using my brain? I didn't have beauty or charm or an inheritance to fall back on!' Her voice was fierce. 'You can't say you admire my mind one minute, then turn round and criticise it when it doesn't suit you to hear what I have to say.' She bent to snap on an extra light, trying like crazy to distract herself and take some of the tension out of the air, but, although an added apricot glow flooded through the room, the tension remained just as high. *Think logically,* she told herself. *Think clearly. Don't hide behind politeness or subterfuge. Tell him the facts so that he can be in no doubt.*

'You don't realise, do you, Zayed,' she said, 'that you think you're offering me everything while in reality you're offering nothing.'

His eyes narrowed. 'Didn't you hear a word of what I just said?'

'I heard you loud and clear. But while companionship and sexual attraction and intellectual stimulation tick many of the boxes necessary for a satisfactory marriage, you've missed out the most important one of all—especially if you want to make it a happy marriage.'

He froze, his body tensing—as if anticipating her next words. As if daring her to say them. 'And you're about to tell me what that is, are you?' he challenged softly.

'You know I am, because it's a fact. And it's called love.' The words exploded from her lips in a way she hadn't anticipated. 'The feeling which defies all logic or reason. Which strikes when you least expect it— and, in my case, when you least want it.' The lump in her throat was making speech difficult but what was even harder was knowing she was opening herself up to him and leaving herself with nowhere to hide. But she had to do it. Something told her she had no choice. 'I didn't want to feel this way but it got me all the same. And I love you, Zayed,' she whispered. 'Despite your arrogance and your outrageousness, I've fallen in love with you.'

Her words died on her lips because his body language had suddenly changed. The analytical part of her had suspected her declaration was going to fall on false ears. But the emotional part—the part which had unwillingly been sucked in and enchanted by the man he truly was beneath the macho exterior—didn't that hold out some flickering hope that he might return her love, even if only a little?

He had moved away to stand by the dying embers of the fire she'd lit earlier. As if in those glowing coals he might find the answer to a question he didn't want to ask. But when he looked up there was no peace or acceptance in his ravaged features. There was anger, yes—and disappointment, too.

'I have offered you everything that I have to offer,' he said. 'And as much of myself as it is possible to give. I have not fed you lies, nor fantasies, Jane. I have made you only the promises I am capable of keeping and if that isn't enough—'

'No,' she said quickly. 'It isn't.'

'Why not?'

She shrugged. 'Don't you know that nature abhors a vacuum? And there would be a huge vacuum in our marriage if such a big thing was missing. If our feelings are so fundamentally *unequal*, it could never work. I would love you far too much, while you would love me not at all. You must know that, Zayed, just as I do. So...' She could feel another lump forming in her throat and she was terrified that she was going to break down and do something stupid. Something unforgivable, like clinging to his leg and begging him to stay. 'I don't really think there's any more to be said, do you? It's been good to clear the air, but you'll probably want to get going now. It's a long drive back.'

There was a loaded pause before he nodded and just before he turned away he looked at her—his eyes full of darkness and regret.

'Goodbye, Jane,' he said, a note in his voice she'd never heard before. Something she didn't recognise. Something which tore at her heart with painful claws.

And that was it. There was no kiss or hug. They might as well have been two strangers. She might as well have been someone at whose door he had just stopped to ask for directions. As suddenly as he'd turned up, he was gone and Jane almost thought she might have imagined it if moments later she hadn't

heard the powerful sound of an engine, or seen the
sweeping arc of headlights as two cars passed the
cottage.

She was trembling for ages after he'd gone, even
though she tried to tell herself she should have been
relieved. Because she had been true to herself, hadn't
she? And to him. Briefly, she found herself wish-
ing he *had* been one of those men who said things
they didn't mean. Who could have told her he loved
her and managed to do a pretty good impression
of loving her. But deep down she knew that would
never have been enough. Her own love would have
swamped them—trapped him and left him wanting to escape.

Walking into the kitchen, she turned on the tap
to pour herself a glass of water, wondering why he
couldn't do love when it was obvious he cared about
her. Why he couldn't go the extra distance and give
her what every woman secretly wanted. And then it
hit her, like an almighty blow to the head, and she
wondered how she could have been so stupid.

She thought about his mother who had loved his
father and had married him, instead of settling for
a marriage of convenience. Because of that love
she had died and Zayed's father had died in trying
to avenge her death. Zayed had been haunted by
nightmares of guilt and remorse, yet after he'd talked
about it those nightmares had stopped. But the con-

sequences hadn't. They just kept on rippling down through the ages. Unless you acknowledged them. If you told yourself that you had enough love for both of them, instead of selfishly demanding your own share.

For it was blindingly simple.

He didn't do love because he associated it with loss.

Fumbling for her phone, Jane punched out Zayed's number but there was nothing but an empty tone in response and she wondered why he'd changed it. Not caring about the time difference, she phoned Hassan in the Kafalahian palace and she could tell from the drowsiness in his voice that he'd been asleep.

'I'm so sorry to disturb you, Hassan,' she babbled. 'But I need Zayed's new number and I need it now.'

'I can't do that, Your Royal Highness. He gave me specific—'

'Hassan, *please*. It's…important.'

There was a pause. 'I may just lose my job over this,' said the aide, with a sigh. 'Have you got a pen?'

But when she dialled the number Zayed didn't answer. Tears slid down her cheeks as she tried again. And again. She knew the signal was notoriously bad in this part of Wales but something told her there was a darker explanation why he wasn't picking up. He didn't want to talk to her. She'd got what she wanted. She'd told him she loved him and he had gone—and she was just going to have to deal with it. Yet something made her punch out the number one last time and she heard it ringing...

Outside her door!

Running across the room, she wrenched it open to find the Sheikh standing there and he took one look at her tear-stained face before pushing her inside, kicking the door shut with his foot before starting to kiss her. He kissed her as she could never remember him having kissed her before. It was a kiss which could have told the whole story of their relationship, full of sorrow and regret and undeniable passion. And as she kissed him back she told herself to be grateful for what she had. Because if this was as good as it got, then who was she to complain?

When at last she felt dizzy from sheer lack of oxygen, she tore her lips away from his. 'Zayed. Listen. I get it. I totally get why you only want an arranged marriage and I'm good with that. Because I want you too much to bear thinking what life without you would be like. I can understand your reasoning perfectly. You don't trust love and why should you? But it doesn't matter,' she said, panting a little. 'It's just a word.'

'No, Jane,' he corrected, with an emphatic shake of his head. 'It isn't just a word, it's a feeling.' He pulled her closer and stared down at her so that their eyes were locked on a collision course. 'It's what has been firing my blood yet filling me with despair in my inability to accept it. I, who am scared of nothing, was scared of the way you made me feel. Make me feel. It came out of somewhere—I don't know where.' He swallowed, his next words leaving his mouth with some difficulty. 'Now at last I understand why my mother defied her country and walked away from an arranged marriage once she met my father. Because if she felt a fraction of what I feel for you—she would have been powerless to do anything else. None of us ever know what the consequences of love will be but that doesn't mean we should ever turn our backs on it.'

'Zayed,' she said breathlessly but he silenced her with a brief shake of his head before starting to speak again.

'All I know is that I don't want to live without you, Jane. For me, that simply isn't an option. That I want to take you back to Kafalah and spend the rest of my life with you. That I want you to have my babies, if destiny wills it. And most important of all, for you to know that I love you and that I will never stop loving you.' His thumbs brushed away the few remaining tears which still lingered on her cheeks. 'Now and for ever.'

And Jane, whose whole life had been governed by her agility and ability with words, for once was completely speechless. She just closed her eyes and briefly gave thanks for this chance at a happiness she'd never believed possible and she vowed to love him with all her heart for as long as she lived. And then she wrapped her arms tightly around his neck and began to kiss him.

EPILOGUE

ZAYED PEERED INTO the crib. The lusty cries of the baby were growing quieter as sleep claimed him and the Sheikh smiled. A curled little fist lay above his son's wavy black hair making him look as if he were about to do battle. Four months old, with a sturdy body more befitting a child almost twice his age— Zayed wondered if his first-born would become a thinker or a warrior. He smiled over at Jane. Or both.

'Tired?' he questioned.

She shook her head, golden-brown hair falling over the shoulders of her sky-blue tunic. 'I had a nap this afternoon. I'm wide awake and raring to go.'

He walked over to lace his fingers in hers and together they went out onto the veranda, which was fragrant with the scent of blooms from the nearby rose garden. It was a clear desert night and the stars looked very big and very close.

He glanced down into his wife's face. Motherhood suited her very well, he thought—for there was a new serenity and a calmness about her which shone from her like the brightest planet in the heavens. Every day, he loved her a little more. She had shown stoicism during her long labour and had wept quiet tears of joy when they'd put the wriggling child to her breast. As had he. She'd told him she planned to take a year off while Malek was still a baby and then planned to resume her work on the definitive study of Kafalah.

Zayed had never known that joy could be so fierce or that love could grow as rampantly as the most vigorous plants in the palace gardens. He had not realised that one woman would be enough for him. More than enough. But then there had been much he had not known before he met Jane.

Who would have guessed that his kingship was made easier with her at his side? Or that her growing confidence and quiet intellect had made her a global sensation? Unlike many women she had not let it go to her head. She had refused all offers for interviews unless it was to draw attention to a worthy cause or to continue in her plans to pioneer the causes of women in the desert region.

She was smiling at him now, lifting on tiptoe so that she could touch her mouth to his, and he traced his tongue along her bottom lip, which trembled in response.

'I love you, my sweet flower of the desert,' he said.

'And I love you too, Zayed Al Zawba.'

He could smell her perfume—more intoxicating than the musky scent of the roses outside. 'When you said you were raring to go,' he murmured, tightening his hands around a waist already slender, despite her having given birth so recently, 'did you have anything particular in mind?'

'I did.' Her voice was a whisper; a soft command. 'Come with me, my masterful Sheikh, and I'll show you exactly what I had in mind.'

Pulling away from him, she flashed him a glance of pure coquetry which made him wonder how the hell she always managed to be so damned provocative. Maybe it was time to show her who was boss. She liked that. And so did he. With a small growl, he picked up his laughing wife and carried her into the bedroom.

* * * * *

If you enjoyed
THE SHEIKH'S BOUGHT WIFE
why not explore these other WEDLOCKED! *titles?*

THE DESERT KING'S CAPTIVE BRIDE
by Annie West
CLAIMED FOR THE DE CARILLO TWINS
by Abby Green
BRIDE BY ROYAL DECREE
by Caitlin Crews
BOUND BY HIS DESERT DIAMOND
by Andie Brock
BABY OF HIS REVENGE BY
Jennie Lucas

Available now!

#3529 SOLD FOR THE GREEK'S HEIR
Brides for the Taking
by Lynne Graham
Jax Antonakos considers a ready-made heir to be worth bidding for—especially if it makes Lucy Dixon his! He's determined to remind Lucy of their insatiable chemistry in the wedding bed—and Lucy finds his claim a struggle to resist...

#3530 THE PRINCE'S CAPTIVE VIRGIN
Once Upon a Seduction...
by Maisey Yates
Ruthless Prince Adam Katsaros offers Belle a deal—he'll release her father if she becomes his mistress! Adam's gaze awakens a heated desire in Belle. Her innocent beauty might redeem his royal reputation—but can she tame the beast inside?

#3531 THE SECRET SANCHEZ HEIR
by Cathy Williams
When Leandro Sanchez uncovers the consequences of his one night with innocent Abigail, she finds herself completely at the billionaire's mercy. The Spanish tycoon *always* gets what he wants, and now he's determined to legitimize his heir...by seducing Abigail into wearing his ring!

#3532 XENAKIS'S CONVENIENT BRIDE
The Secret Billionaires
by Dani Collins
Stavros Xenakis refuses to marry—until deliciously tempting Calli proves that a wife is exactly what he needs! Stavros's proposal gives Calli the chance to find her stolen son. But she doesn't expect life as Mrs. Xenakis to be quite so satisfying...

Get 2 Free Books,
Plus 2 Free Gifts—
just for trying the Reader Service!

*Ruthless Prince Adam Katsaros offers Belle a deal—
he'll release her father if she becomes his mistress!
Adam's gaze awakens a heated desire in Belle. Her
innocent beauty might redeem his royal reputation—but
can she tame the beast inside...?*

Read on for a sneak preview of
THE PRINCE'S CAPTIVE VIRGIN,
the first part of **Maisey Yates**'s
ONCE UPON A SEDUCTION... *trilogy.*

"You really are kind of a beast," Belle said, standing up.
Adam caught her wrist, stopped her from leaving.

"And what bothers you most about that? The fact that
you would like to reform me, that you would like for your
time here to mean something and you are beginning to
see that it won't? Or is it the fact that you don't want to
reform me at all, and that you rather like me this way? Or
at least, your body likes me this way."

"Bodies make stupid decisions all the time. My father
wanted my mother, and she was a terrible, unloving person
who didn't even want her own daughter. So, forgive me if
I find this argument rather uncompelling. It doesn't make
you a good person, just because I enjoy kissing you. And
it doesn't make this something worth exploring."

She broke free of him and began to walk away, striding
down the hall, back toward her room. He pushed away
from the table, letting his chair fall to the floor, not caring
enough to right it as he followed after Belle.

He caught up to her, pivoting so that he was in front of her. She took a step backward, then to the side, butting up against the wall. Then he caged her between his arms, staring down at her. Her blue eyes were glittering, her breasts rising and falling rapidly with each breath.

"This is the only thing worth exploring. Not what could be, but what you have. The fire that burns between you and another person. For all you know, in the days since you've been here the entire world has fallen away. And if we were all that was left…would you not regret missing out on the chance to see how hot we could burn?"

She shook her head. "But the world hasn't fallen away," she said, her trembling lips pale now, a complete contrast to the rich color they had been only moments ago. "It's still there. And whatever happens in here will have consequences out there. I will help you, Adam, but I'm not going to give you my body. I'm not going to destroy that life that I have out there to play games with you in here. You're a stranger to me, and you're going to remain a stranger to me. I can pretend. I can give you whatever you need when it comes to making a statement for your country. But beyond that? I can't."

Then she turned and walked away, and this time, he let her go.

Don't miss
THE PRINCE'S CAPTIVE VIRGIN
available June 2017 wherever
Harlequin Presents® books and ebooks are sold.

www.Harlequin.com

HARLEQUIN
Presents®

**Next month, look out for *The Prince's Nine-Month Scandal*
by Caitlin Crews, the first part of her sinfully exciting new
duet, Scandalous Royal Brides!**

Natalie and Valentina cannot believe their eyes…they're the very
image of one another, so similar they could be identical twins. They
agree to swap identities for six weeks—but what will happen when
the alpha heroes closest to them uncover the outrageous truth?

Natalie Monette's life is transformed by meeting Valentina—but
Valentina is unhappily engaged to the supremely arrogant Crown
Prince Rodolfo. Natalie's plan is to put arrogant Rodolfo in his
place…until she's enticed by the heat between them!

Prince Rodolfo can't understand why, having *never* felt any desire
for his betrothed, he now can't keep his hands off this captivating
woman. But scandal abounds when he discovers who he's shared
such passion with…and that she's carrying his heir!

Don't miss

The Prince's Nine-Month Scandal

Available June 2017

And discover Princess Valentina and Achilles Casilieris's story

The Billionaire's Secret Princess

Available July 2017

Stay Connected:

www.Harlequin.com

🅵 /HarlequinBooks

🐦 @HarlequinBooks

🅟 /HarlequinBooks

HP06068